Estelle's Endeavor

By Linda Shenton Matchett

Estelle's Endeavor
By Linda Shenton Matchett

Cover Design by: Cover art by Randi Gammons, Randi Gammons Graphic Design. Branding for series by Carpe Librum Book Design

ISBN: 978-1-7363256-3-6

Published by Shortwave Press

*To my mom, who passed onto Glory
while I was writing this story.
She was one of my biggest cheerleaders.
This one's for you, Mom.*

Chapter One

Estelle Johnson hurried up the front stairs to the public library, the morning newspaper filled with the latest casualty lists and battle reports tucked under her arm. Having overslept again after a fitful night, she hadn't had time to check for Aubry's name or that of any of their friends. Heart pounding, she bit back a sob. Surely, if he was injured or worse, she would have heard something. Had his mother received one of those dreaded black-edged telegrams by a uniformed man on a bike and not telephoned?

She stopped in front of the door, lifted her chin, and squared her shoulders. Despite the uncertainties of the war, Mrs. Ryskamp, the library director, would expect her to be cheerful and welcoming to their patrons. They came into the building to escape the daily difficulties of rationing, making do, and waiting for letters from loved ones. She pinned on a smile, then opened the door and marched to the circulation desk where her coworker looked up and scowled. The woman rarely had a kind word for Estelle since she'd started as a circulation assistant. A year of silent sneers and not-so-silent snide comments. What had she done to annoy the woman?

Swallowing, Estelle broadened her smile. "Good morning, Francine. How are you this morning?"

Eyes glittering, the woman shrugged. "As well as can be expected, having to drag the book return to the desk by myself. I suppose you have a good reason for being late."

With a glance at the clock on the wall, Estelle schooled her features. "I'm ten minutes early and would gladly have helped, if you'd waited." She lifted the hinged section of the counter and slipped past the woman. "I'll put away my things and be out to give you a hand unless you have another task you prefer me to do."

"Suit yourself." Francine grabbed a book from the wooden crate and dropped it on the gleaming surface with a resounding thud. "Makes no difference to me what you do."

Pressing her lips together, Estelle walked through the doorway that led to the offices and tiny room the staff members used to take their breaks. Unsurprisingly, the rooms were dark. Francine typically kept her jibes to herself unless the director or other staff weren't in the building.

Estelle tucked her purse and the newspaper into her assigned cubby, with a sigh. She wouldn't be able to peruse the periodical until lunch. Hopefully, the library would be busy and cause the hours to fly instead of crawl. She fingered the paper and pursed her lips. *Please, God, let it be filled with good news for a change.*

Footsteps sounded, and the director appeared on the threshold, a small, brown hat perched on her snow-white hair coiffed in an elegant chiffon. Her pocketbook strap was slung over one shoulder. Although several years out of date, her tan suit appeared brand new. "Good morning, Estelle."

"Good morning, Mrs. Ryskamp. Is there anything special you'd like me to work on today?" Had she been in the building when Francine made her disparaging remarks?

The older woman's expression lit up. "As a matter of fact, I've got the perfect job for you. At last night's meeting, the trustees and I discussed holding a book sale sometime this summer. You're so creative, I thought you should spearhead the event."

"Me?" Estelle's voice came out as a squeak, and she cleared her throat. "Uh, what about Francine? She's been here longer than me."

"Her gifts are better utilized elsewhere." Mrs. Ryskamp squeezed Estelle's shoulder. "Review the stacks, and make a list of books we might consider selling, then come up with a plan for the event."

"A plan?" Estelle smoothed her skirt. The woman would think her a ninny with her one-word answers. "Did you have a date in mind?"

"Not specifically, but perhaps in August when things are winding down. Rather than using the event as a fundraiser for the library, bring us suggestions for a cause we can support for the war effort. Let's consider making it more than a sale. Perhaps add readings or book discussions." Mrs. Ryskamp removed her hat, then patted her pristine hair and grinned. "The sky's the limit, my girl. War is serious business, but it can't go on much longer. I feel it in my bones. As awful as the landings at Normandy were, the boys seem to be making progress and pushing those Germans back on their heels. We need to cheer up the patrons and prepare ourselves for when our sons, brothers, and fathers return. This will be just the ticket."

"Yes, ma'am. I'll get right on it. I won't let you down."

"You never do. Now, scoot before Francine gets any more sour."

Warmth filling her, Estelle nodded.

"I'm well aware of her difficult nature, dear, and I appreciate your professionalism in dealing with her. I'm not at liberty to share, but she's had a hard life. Sometimes that makes a person bitter."

"Yes, ma'am," Estelle repeated. "And thank you for your faith in me." She strode down the corridor and into the library. Francine placed the last of the returned books on the wheeled wooden cart, the metal one having been donated to the scrap pile in the early days after Pearl Harbor. She took a deep breath. "May I shelve the books for you, Francine? Unless you have a mind to do it."

Face scrunched as if she'd eaten a lemon, Francine glared at her. "I suppose you think offering to help will get in good with Mrs. Ryskamp," she hissed. "Well, it won't work. She'll see who you really are at some point."

Her stomach roiled, and Estelle stepped back as if slapped. What *was* the woman's problem? Straightening her spine, she wrapped her fingers around the cart handle. "I'm not sure what I've done to deserve your censure, Francine, but I'd appreciate it if you'd treat me with respect. I've been nothing but nice to you. If you can't curb your nastiness, please don't speak to me unless you have a question."

The woman's haughtiness faltered, and her eyes clouded, but no apology was forthcoming. She turned away and busied herself with something under the desk.

Estelle rolled the cart toward the shelves, tears pricking the backs of her eyes. Her heart threatened to jump from her chest. Her morning devotion had been about showing kindness to her enemy. Instead, she'd lectured Francine about her behavior. Had the woman deserved to be chided? Perhaps, but that's not what the Bible passage said to do. *Forgive me, Lord. Help me make things right with Francine. Help me curb my own tongue.*

She sorted the books into Dewey decimal order, then trundled down the aisles and returned the volumes to their rightful places. Her pulse slowed as she immersed herself in the soothing rhythm of the job. Thirty minutes later, she'd finished, so she wheeled the cart into the closet where it would remain until closing time. Bracing herself for more ugliness, she strode to the circulation desk to retrieve a notebook and pencil, but Francine was nowhere in sight.

With a quick motion, she grabbed the supplies and hurried back to the stacks. She cringed at her cowardly actions. She'd be brave and gracious later. Much later.

Starting with the fiction collection, she ran her finger down each spine, then noted duplicates in the pad. She flipped open older novels to determine the last time they'd been checked out. Her list grew as did her excitement for the money they would raise for a worthy cause. There were so many.

She moved on to the nonfiction section. Her stomach rumbled, and she glanced at the watch pinned to her bodice. Nearly noon. No wonder she was hungry. Although anxious to check the newspaper, she'd give Francine her break first. A step toward mending fences.

"Franci—" Estelle's pulse skittered. Aubry's mother stood in front of the desk, her face wan and pinched, her hands clutching a telegram. Even Francine looked rattled. Estelle rushed forward. "What's happened? He's not—" She couldn't bring herself to verbalize the terrible word.

"No, child, he's not dead." Tears dampened Mrs. DeLuca's cheeks. "He's been injured, but I don't know how badly. I don't know anything." Her hand shook as she gave Estelle the tiny envelope. "All it says is that he was wounded and is in a hospital somewhere, that more information will be forthcoming." Her tone was wooden as she quoted the cable.

Pinpricks of light danced in Estelle's vision, and she swayed. Gripping the counter, she willed herself to remain on her feet. She couldn't faint. Not now. Not in front of Aubry's mother, who obviously needed support. Having been widowed while he was in high school, she was alone.

"We'll get through this, Mrs. DeLuca." Estelle put one arm around the woman's shoulder. "We'll get through this together, and I'll help you chase down the information." She glanced at her coworker. "And perhaps Francine can help us. She's a wizard at research."

Francine's eyes widened as her gaze shot between Estelle and Mrs. DeLuca, then she lifted her chin. "Uh, yes. I'd be happy to provide assistance. We'll get you the answers you seek."

Estelle nibbled the inside of her cheek. Did she want the information?

CHAPTER TWO

Footsteps echoed in the hallway outside his room, and Aubry DeLuca strained to listen. Would they come inside? Would the bandages that cloaked his eyes finally be removed? Did he want to know the extent of damage done to his vision?

With a sigh, he shifted in the bed, and pain shot up his leg. Biting back a moan, he grimaced. Shrapnel had sliced through the muscle in his thigh, leaving him with a gash that required more than thirty stitches, to say nothing of the work inside the surgeon had to do. But thanks to the man's expertise, Aubry would only have only a slight limp after he finished therapy.

Voices sounded, then faded. He wrestled with the sheets, damp with his sweat. What time was it? Living in perpetual darkness meant he had no idea if it was day or night, although the amount of activity seemed to indicate it was daytime.

"Stop flopping around like a fish on the beach." The sardonic tones of his roommate Roger Valnicek split the silence. "You're worse than a three-year-old in church."

"You still here?" Aubry frowned. "I thought I had the place to myself."

"No such luck, my friend. You've got me and three of your closest friends to keep you company."

"At least I won't be lonely." Sarcasm dripped from his voice.

Roger snickered. "Not with me around."

"Sensitive as always."

"How bad is the pain? I was teasing to try to get your mind off it."

"You'd make a wonderful nurse." Aubry grinned. Roger was a good guy. Always ready with a joke or a smile, his antics had kept up the platoon's morale. "But I don't think you have the gams for the uniform."

Snorting a laugh, Roger said, "Maybe the patients would like that hairy gorilla look. You never know."

"Trust me, I know." His thigh throbbed, and Aubry fisted his hands. The therapist had pushed him harder than usual yesterday, claiming he was well on his way to mending and had been babying the injury. What did the guy know about combat wounds? He'd spent the war safely tucked in a hospital behind the lines. "When do you get sprung?"

"Soon. The doc says I'm almost good as new."

"Really?" Aubry's pulse sped up. "They sending you back?"

"Nah. They decided they could do without me."

Something in his friend's voice told Aubry there was more to the story. How badly had Roger been injured? Were his eyes bandaged, too? Dare he ask?

"All right, gentlemen, time for breakfast." The orderly's shoes squeaked on the wooden floor as he entered the room. The tangy aroma of sausage and sweet smell of syrup filled the room.

Aubry's mouth watered. There was nothing wrong with his appetite. Despite the discomfort of his injuries, he hadn't lost his desire for food. The doc had said that was a good sign. Said Aubry needed to put on the weight he'd lost leading up to battle. Nerves made his stomach clench, so keeping food down had been a challenge. Then the fighting began, and the carnage stripped away any remaining hunger he might have felt.

Memories washed over him, and he shoved them away. He couldn't do anything for his friends, so he needed to forget them. Forget what happened. More images invaded. Why couldn't he make his brain do what he commanded?

"Do you need help sitting up, Captain DeLuca?"

A hand came to rest on Aubry's shoulder, and he waved it away. "I may not be able to see, but I'm not helpless."

"Yes, sir."

"Lighten up, DeLuca. The man is here with your food. No need to be peevish with him."

"You're right. I'm sorry."

"No need to apologize, sir. I can't relate, but I'm sure you're frustrated at not being able to see. I'll open the window before I leave to sweep away some of the stuffiness."

Aubry sat up, then propped his pillow behind his back. Yanking on the sheet, he pulled it up to his chin, leaving his arms on top of the fabric. "Thank you. Any chance of getting out of this place later? I'm sure you folks are busy."

"Not too busy to get you and your friend outside. I'll check your schedule."

"Yes, I might be booked solid for the afternoon." Aubry shot a smile in the direction he thought the man was standing. "I'm very important, you know."

The orderly chuckled and set a tray on Aubry's lap. "Sausage is at ten o'clock, juice is at one o'clock, and your pancakes are smack-dab in the middle of your plate. I hope you like syrup; the cook was a little zealous."

"Better than being stingy."

"True." The man squeezed Aubry's forearm, then walked away, presumably to serve Roger. Moments later, the window rattled, and a warm, floral-scented breeze caressed Aubry's cheeks. Then the orderly's footsteps and the whisper of the wheels on his cart faded.

With tentative fingers, Aubry explored his tray based on the man's description of where his food was on the plate. Using the layout of a clock was clever and worked perfectly. He knew the exact location of each item. He gripped the glass, then took a deep drink of orange juice. Tepid and not very flavorful, the liquid soothed his throat nonetheless. He found his knife and fork and stabbed at where he hoped the sausage resided. The utensil met with resistance, and he smirked. He was getting pretty good at playing pin-the-tail-on-the-donkey with his food.

He poked the sausage link into his mouth and chewed. Delicious. Who knew the army could provide decent food sometimes?

Silverware clinked on china across the room, and the men ate in silence. Birdsong sounded outside, then the occasional laughter or murmur of conversation. The tightness in Aubry's chest eased as he let his mind wander home, to pickup games of kickball and baseball. Sun shining and humidity thick as soup, typical for a Maryland summer day, but he and the other kids never seemed to mind.

Nibbling on the syrup-drenched pancakes, he reminisced about lazy days near the river, fishing pole gripped in one hand. He'd never managed to talk Estelle into joining him. She was a good sport, but piercing a worm on a hook and dunking a line into the water didn't appeal to her.

Estelle. Had she received word of his injuries? Three weeks had passed since Normandy, and ten days since he'd been transported to the rehab hospital, yet he hadn't received any letters from her. Was it a case of the army not delivering his mail, or had she run for the hills after hearing about his wounds? He wouldn't blame her if she did.

He dropped his utensils on the tray, then wiped his mouth on the napkin. He hadn't written, either. What was there to say? Dear Estelle, I'm not quite the man you knew.

"Enough of that?" Roger's voice pierced his thoughts.

Aubry turned toward his friend. "Enough of what?"

"Feelin' sorry for yourself. I see the way you're looking. You're thinking about your girl." Roger sighed. "You can't go there. I know you haven't heard from her, but there's probably a very good reason that has to do with the army and its ability to keep a man waiting for his mail."

"Yeah, I considered that, but what if I'm wrong? What if she decides she wants a man who's whole? There are going to be plenty of guys who don't go home missing parts."

"That's not you."

"Maybe. The doc says I have to be realistic about my vision. Or lack thereof."

"Being blind wouldn't be the worst thing to happen."

A chill washed over Aubry, and he pursed his lips. In the days since arriving, he'd been so focused on himself, he hadn't asked Roger about his injuries. He had to be in bad shape if he was still here at the hospital. He took a deep breath. "I've been a total jerk not asking about you, Roger. It's not that the army can do without you, is it? You were hurt bad, weren't you?"

Silence.

"Roger? I'm sorry for being so selfish."

"I donated an arm to the cause." Roger's voice held false bravado. "Tough to shoot if you can't get a good grip on the rifle."

"Oh, buddy, I'm so sorry."

"No need to apologize, friend. I've had some time to get used to the idea. Can't say I'm happy that God allowed me to be maimed, but He and I have had lots of conversations, and I'm coming around. I'd like to see my wife and kids again, and He's gonna let me do that."

"They know?"

"Yep, and Marilyn says she can't wait to see me. And her letter sounds like she means it. Not gonna cut me any slack, either. She included a list of stuff she wants me to do when I get home."

"You've got a winner, Roger."

"That I do."

More footsteps and the swish of a nurse's skirts. Hands removed the tray from his lap, then the doctor's voice broke into their conversation. "Time to remove your bandages, Captain DeLuca."

Chapter Three

Early morning sunlight seeped between the curtains in Estelle's room as she sat up in the bed and stretched. Groggy from a fitful night, she yawned broadly. Her eyes felt as gritty as if she'd been in a sandstorm, and her forehead throbbed. What a blessing that today was her day off from work. She'd be very little use to anyone, and she didn't need to give Francine another opportunity to criticize her. The woman had actually mumbled a few words resembling condolences after Mrs. DeLuca came in with the telegram, but her expression belied the sentiment, although she had agreed to track down Aubry's location.

Estelle rotated her neck to ease the tightness in her shoulder muscles, but they refused to relax. She squinted at the clock on the nightstand and flopped against the mattress. Five forty-five. No need to rise yet, although the muffled sounds of her mother fixing breakfast tempted her to swing her feet to the floor and don her robe. She curled into a ball on her side and watched shadows dance on the wall.

What was Aubry looking at right now? Where was he? Somewhere in Europe? Had he made it to the States yet? Why would the

Army send a telegram with just enough information to upset everyone? How hard would it be to include everything loved ones needed to know?

Too many questions and no answers.

A sigh escaped, and she closed her eyes. *Lord, You hold Aubry in Your hands, so I know he's being watched over, but please don't keep Mrs. DeLuca and me waiting too long for news. I know worry is a sin, but I can't help being anxious. Please take away any pain he has. Heal him.*

Yesterday, Mrs. Ryskamp had given Estelle the rest of the day off to be with Mrs. DeLuca. They'd gone to the newspaper office, but the trip had been a waste of time. None of the reporters were able to tell them anything not already in the paper. The town clerk's office had been more helpful giving them the address and phone number to the Office of War Information, but by the time she'd accompanied Mrs. DeLuca home, it was too late to call.

Not that the OWI would have specific news about Aubry, but they would know who to contact. She'd decided in the middle of the night that she'd consider boarding the bus to DC and marching into the front lobby. Surely, they'd have to provide assistance if she showed up in person.

Distraught, Mrs. DeLuca barely ate the simple meal Estelle had put together, then they'd spent hours on the couch looking through photo albums. A bittersweet night. She and Aubry weren't close enough before he left to peruse pictures of his childhood, so she enjoyed watching him grow from a cute little boy to a handsome man, but seeing him whole and unharmed was difficult.

Did he lose a limb? Many of the men who came home through Fort Meade had pinned-up sleeves or trouser legs. Was he scarred? How did he *feel*? How did any of them feel after being handed guns and told to shoot men they had no beef with. Hitler was a monster, but did all German soldiers believe his terrible philosophies, or were they drafted like the boys and men from the US?

Could she look at Aubry day after day if he wasn't the same man who'd boarded the bus for the base? *Oh, Lord, please give me strength.*

Huffing a sigh, Estelle sat up. Attempting to sleep was an exercise in futility. May as well get started on the day. She padded to the closet and yanked the nearest dress off the hanger, then walked to the bureau to obtain her underclothes. She trudged down the hall to the bathroom. Hopefully, standing under a stream of hot water would wash away the wooziness. Convinced of the health benefits of a shower touted by magazines, her parents had one installed in '38. She didn't know if what the article said was true, but the steam and jets of water typically soothed her like nothing else.

Twenty minutes later, she was clean and refreshed. Ready to face whatever came, she straightened her spine and opened the door. The savory aroma of bacon wafted from below, and her mouth watered. Her stomach gurgled. Nothing wrong with her appetite, apparently. She hurried to her room, tossed her nightgown into the hamper, then poked her feet into a pair of low-heeled pumps. She grabbed her pocketbook and coat, then descended the stairs and went to the kitchen.

Estelle's mother stood at the stove, scooping creamy, yellow curds of scrambled eggs onto a platter. Her father sat at the table behind the morning edition of the newspaper. His forehead wrinkled as he peeked over the paper at her. "I'd hope you'd sleep in, sweetie."

She picked up the plate of bacon and set it on the table before dropping into her seat. "I tried, but..." She shrugged and put the ivory-colored cloth napkin in her lap. "I'm going into the city to see what I can unearth."

"Would you like company?" Her father folded the paper and laid it next to his plate. "No one would miss me if I took the day off."

"I find that hard to believe." Estelle put a piece of toast on her plate.

"Will you be home before dark?" Her mother set the eggs on the table, then seated herself. "DC is a dangerous place with all those workers who have flooded the city."

Extending his arms to the women, her father winked at Estelle. "Let's pray for our girl's safety, Norma. And for this delicious food. Then we can talk." After a brief blessing, her father released her fingers and picked up his fork. "Dig in, ladies."

Estelle bit into the crispy strip of bacon, and the meat's salted, smoky flavor exploded on her tongue. She swallowed, then looked at her father. "Do you think Mr. Martin would give you the day off, Daddy? Whether I like it or not, you're more apt to get answers than me." She rolled her eyes. "Authorities don't tend to take young women seriously. Look how long it's taken companies to hire us to do men's jobs."

20

"Give them some grace." He winked. "There are a couple of centuries of customs to change, but yes, the aircraft factory will be fine if I miss a day. Family comes first."

"Thanks, Daddy." She could always count on him. He never wavered and supported her in every way, no matter what. Could she do that for Aubry?

CHAPTER FOUR

Rain pummeled the roof, and thunder boomed. Aubry flinched. Not being able to see the lightning prevented him from anticipating the explosive sounds. Too much like combat. Whimpering mingled with the storm, and nurses circulated among the beds murmuring soft assurances to the men. His lips twisted. It would take more than kind words and a gentle hand to push away the sights, sounds, and smells of battle.

"Close your eyes, Captain DeLuca. I've lowered the lights, but we want to give your eyes time to adjust."

Hearting pounding, Aubry did as he was told. Was the rain God's way of warning him that his vision was gone? That He mourned with him?

The steel of the scissors was cold against his skin as the doctor snipped away the dressing. He unwrapped the bandage from around Aubry's head, then plucked the circles of gauze off his eyes. "Open your eyes slowly, Captain."

Aubry cracked his eyelids, then slammed them shut as light pierced his vision, and knifelike agony shot through his head. He tried again, and this time no pain accompanied the action. His eyelids fluttered. A face came into view, blurry and wavering, but at least he could see something. He grinned and brought his hand toward his face to rub away the clouds from his sight, but the doctor halted the motion.

"It will take time to clear, and rubbing won't solve anything."

"Yes, sir." He continued to blink, but the edges of the man's image refused to sharpen. And it was as if Aubry was only looking at half a picture.

The doctor pulled a tiny flashlight from his white coat.

A chill coursed through Aubry's veins, and he forced his eyes to remain open. "What is it?"

"Lie still. I need to check your pupils' response." With a gentle touch, the doctor rested a finger on each of Aubry's eyelids and waved the pinpoint of light: first, up and down, then back and forth, before stowing the implement. "I'm pleased to report you have response in your right eye." He cleared his throat. "However, you've lost the sight in your left eye, and there's nothing I can do."

"What? Why?" Aubry clenched his fists. "What do you mean you can't do anything? You're a surgeon, aren't you?"

"Yes, but there are limitations to science. You sustained physical damage to the eye that I was hoping would heal. Unfortunately, that hasn't occurred, and your pupil is completely clouded over."

"Isn't there something that can be done? Medicine of some sort?"

"I'm sorry, son." The doctor squeezed Aubry's shoulder. "I won't waste your time with platitudes or false hope. This is difficult, to be sure, but you do have vision in one eye. That's more than some of these boys can say."

"But you're still fuzzy. It's as if I'm looking through a clouded windshield." He turned his head and strained to look at objects in the room. "All I can see is lumps and figures without form."

"That may clear up with time. As I said, your pupil responded, albeit a bit sluggishly." The doctor went to the end of the bed and pulled the clipboard off the hook hanging from the footboard of the cot. He glanced at the sheet of paper, scribbled a few words, then returned the clipboard to the hook. "I'll have the nurse come by to change the dressing on your leg. That wound is healing quite nicely. You should be pleased. You may have a slight limp, but that remains to be seen."

"What does it matter how well I can walk if I can't see?" Aubry couldn't keep the bitterness from his voice. "I'll be no good to anyone."

"Nonsense, young man." The doctor rocked on his heels. "Your value doesn't rest on your capabilities or usefulness. You are a creature of God. He made each of us special and unique, and we have value as one of His creations."

Aubry crossed his arms and frowned. "You missed your calling, Doc; you should have been a preacher."

"Frankly, I considered it, but He had other plans for me."

"Oh." Aubry's face heated. His mother had raised him to be polite, no matter what, but her teachings hadn't prepared him for this. "I...uh—"

"Listen, I haven't experienced a terrible injury such as yours, so I'm not going to insult you by saying I understand how you feel, but I know you're devastated at the moment. You're facing an unknown future, with an unknown outcome, but you *can* overcome this situation. It will be hard, maybe the hardest thing you've ever done, but I have faith in you. And I'll be praying."

"I appreciate you giving it to me straight, Doc, and but I'm not sure God is listening to mankind right now. Why would he allow this war? This terrible, *godforsaken* war?"

"I can't answer that, but He is in charge, and He has his reasons. I have to cling to that. I suggest you do, too." The doctor patted Aubry's ankle. "I've got other rounds to make, but I'll see you before you leave."

"Leave?" Aubry's pulse raced, and his mouth dried. "Am I going...home?"

"Not yet, but you will be going to the States. I'm sending you to Walter Reed. They'll continue to work with you on your leg, and they may be able to do more with your eye. Don't get your hopes up, but they're the army's flagship medical center. If anyone can improve your sight, it's them."

"How long?"

"You're shipping out this afternoon, well, actually flying, but I don't know how long they'll keep you at Reed. Could be weeks, could be days."

"I'm from Maryland, Doc. That's music to my ears."

"Excellent. Take care, son." The doctor gestured to Aubry. "Nurse, he's leaving soon, so he needs his dressing changed now."

"Yes, sir."

Aubry clenched his fists as the woman walked toward him, her shoes squeaking on the wooden floor. He wouldn't miss that sound.

"Congratulations on heading to your next stop." Her touch was light as she cut away the gauze.

He grunted. He was going to another hospital, not much different from this one. So much to take in. He couldn't see. He might never have clear vision again. But he was going home. For him, the war was over. But he'd lost too many friends. Men who'd fought by his side, only to make the greatest sacrifice. But would it be better to have died, than to go through life as a blind cripple?

As the nurse finished, an orderly appeared. "I'd say it's time for a spin around the halls. You've been trapped in this room long enough, eh?"

"Sent you to cheer me up, did they? I'm fine where I am." Aubry knew he was being petulant, but he didn't care. His prognosis was dire, and the guy thought being wheeled through the sterile corridors of the hospital would solve everything? Hardly.

"Nope, I'm here of my own accord." He held up a cane and robe. "I'm Mitch, and a change of scenery will do you good."

"Scenery. Ha! I can't see."

"Nice try, but I happen to know you've got some vision." Mitch shoved a robe into Aubry's hands. "Put that on. As attractive as your pj's are, we're going with formal wear."

"Thanks, but I'm not interested, and your attempts at humor are poor at best."

Mitch shrugged. "I'm an orderly, not a comedian."

"I can attest to that." Aubry blew out a sigh and tossed the garment on the end of the cot. "And I'm really not in the mood for a walk."

"Too bad." Mitch picked up the robe. "Until you're on your own, we get to tell you what to do, and right now, you're going to take a stroll, so put on the robe."

"You're not going to leave me alone, are you?"

"Nope."

"You don't understand what I'm going through—"

"How do you know that?" The man's voice was like steel.

"Uh, well, you're working in a hospital."

"Making assumptions is dangerous, Captain."

"You—"

"Went there and left a leg behind." Mitch tapped Aubry's shoulder with the cane. "Now, put on the robe, take the cane, and get out of bed."

Face burning, Aubry slid his arms into the cotton garment, then reached for the walking stick. "I, um, I'm sorry for being such a dolt."

"You're not the first guy to think I'm a conscientious objector or medic trying to take the easy way out." He crooked his elbow. "Grab on to me, and we'll take this slow. No need to pitch you on your face during your inaugural tour. Then we can talk about the letter you're going to write to your girl."

"Now, who's making assumptions?"

"Me, but experience tells me, she's the reason you're so angry. You wouldn't be as upset if you were going home to Mom and Dad."

Aubry's thigh throbbed, and he winced. "What am I gonna tell her? She's not going to want half a man. I think I should send her a Dear Jane."

CHAPTER FIVE

Breathless, Estelle raced up the stairs to her bedroom, kicked off her shoes, and sank into the rocking chair by the window. She pressed the V-mail envelope to her chest and heaved out a sigh. Aubry was well enough to write. Surely that meant his injuries were not extensive. How long since he'd crafted the letter? Was he back on the lines?

With trembling hands, she slid a finger under the flap. She pulled out the single sheet of paper, then unfolded it. Tears sprang to her eyes at the sight of his familiar handwriting. Even more cramped on the tiny missive that had been reduced onto microfilm, then printed before being delivering to her. What other wonders of technology had come about because of the war?

She stroked the words, then looked at the date. Another sigh, then she brought the letter close to her face to read the miniscule print.

Dear Estelle,

How are you? I can't believe over two years have passed since we said goodbye at the bus station. I don't think I could have gotten through this war without your letters. Some of the guys rarely get mail, so I share your news from home with them.

I guess by now you know I got hurt. You would have been the first one Mom told after getting the telegram. I'm glad you're there for each other.

There are plenty of guys who were injured worse than me, so I guess I should be grateful. Some of the newspapers are touting us as heroes, making it sound like the battle was easy, that we pushed back the Germans with little effort. Hardly. It was hours of brutal fighting. I can still hear the awful sounds and feel the sand under my boots. I don't think I'll ever be able to visit the seaside ever again.

By now, you're probably wishing I'd get to the point. You're wondering how badly I've been wounded. Not as bad as I could have been. My leg will heal, and the doc says I might have a limp, but the rest, well, only time will tell. So, I'm not coming home the same man who left you. More than half but definitely not whole. Anyway, I'm not going to hold you to your promise to wait for me. It wouldn't be fair. You should find another guy. You'll be happier if you do, and I won't blame you.

Aubry

A sob burst from Estelle's lips as she dropped the letter to the floor. More than half? He hadn't revealed the extent of his injuries, but to hear him tell it, he was in bad shape. He hadn't mentioned his arms. Had he lost one? Both? No, he wrote the letter. She'd recognize his handwriting anywhere. So, he had retained his right arm. What about his other leg? Or some other type of wound?

Joel Upchurch had come home disfigured from an explosion. No one had seen him since he returned, and his mother had asked for prayer at church because he'd secreted himself in his room, rarely leaving, and snarling at her most of the time. Was that Aubry's injury? Had he somehow been burned? Or had he been cut up by shrapnel like Lydia's boyfriend, Tristan. The poor man had a jagged scar that ran from his jaw to his temple and many more underneath his clothes, by all reports.

She shuddered. Could she love a man who was maimed? Should she do what he said and find another guy?

An image of the two of them strolling the sidewalks window shopping floated into her mind. Hands clasped together, his palm warm in hers. Taller than her, but not too tall, he looked down at her with a broad grin and sparkling gray eyes. His black hair had a blue sheen in the sunshine. She couldn't remember what he teased her about that day, but she did remember the feeling of being special. He'd looked at her as if she were the only girl in the world.

A thunderstorm had arrived out of nowhere, or perhaps they'd been so caught up in each other they hadn't noticed the darkening skies. Either way, they were surprised at the water pouring down on them and ducked into a nearby shop to escape. It had been a bookstore, and they learned of each other's love of the written word. Recommending books and reading together quickly became their favorite pastime.

Oh, God, please tell me what to do.

A muffled knock sounded on the front door, and she whipped up her head. Had Mrs. DeLuca come calling? Had she received a letter, too? Did she have more information?

Estelle jumped up and checked her appearance in the mirror. No matter what was happening, her mother expected her to look her best. She patted the stray hairs into place, then refreshed her lipstick. Smoothing her skirt, she straightened her spine and marched out of the room.

Voices wafted toward her as she traversed the hallway. From the top of the stairs, she caught sight of Mrs. Feeney through the screen door. Estelle's shoulders slumped, but it would be rude to return to her room. She descended the stairs as the older woman entered the house.

Fine lines were etched on her face, and her snow-white hair was pulled into a simple chignon. Her green dress brought out the green in her hazel eyes that shimmered with unshed tears. An encouraging smile brightened her expression. "Estelle, I heard about Aubry's injury from Irene DeLuca, and came for a visit. I hope you won't think it's an imposition."

Sensing her mother's razor-sharp gaze behind her, Estelle shook her head. "Of course not. I could prepare some tea, and we can sit in the living room."

Mrs. Feeney waved one hand. "No need to go to a lot of trouble, my dear."

"All right." Estelle sent a questioning glance at her mother, who kissed the older woman's cheek, then headed toward the kitchen.

Apparently, Estelle was on her own. She led the woman into the living room, then waited while Mrs. Feeney seated herself on the sofa, before dropping into a nearby chair. "Thank you for coming to see me."

"I should have been here sooner, but Mr. Feeney and I were away. You must be distraught, confused, and angry, just to name some of the emotions rolling around inside you. I wanted to let you know I'm praying for you."

Estelle's eyes widened. Someone who understood. Her breath whooshed out. "Yes, I don't know what to feel, and today I received a letter from him that has made things worse. He wants me to find someone else."

Mrs. Feeney leaned forward and squeezed Estelle's arm. "He thinks he's doing you a favor. He doesn't want to be a burden."

"But if we love each other—"

"Exactly, but he's a mess right now. Not just physically, but mentally, emotionally, and probably spiritually. He's railing at God for letting this happen and questioning why." Mrs. Feeney's eyes took on a distant stare, then she focused on Estelle. "I say all this because I've been where you are. Mr. Feeney was in the Spanish-American war. We'd been married almost ten years, but he felt it was his duty to go, so he enlisted. I tried to stop him, but to no avail. He was a doctor and wanted to do his bit, as they say, to help those young men, so off he went. Near the end of the war, he was shot in the arm, and the wound became infected, terribly so. He thought he was going to lose the limb. Fortunately, that didn't happen, but for weeks the situation was touch and go. He wrote me numerous letters from the hospital in Cuba, begging me to get on with my life. To grant him a divorce, of all things."

"How awful." Estelle's hand flew to her throat as a tear trickled down her cheek. "Obviously, you didn't split up, but it must have been difficult. Thank you for sharing your experience."

"It was hard, but we are stronger for it. You will need to search deep in your heart to determine how you feel. Can you love him as he is? Not pity, but true love. Loving the man on the inside, not the outside. You must pray like you've never prayed before to seek answers from our heavenly Father, and search the scriptures. He will guide you, but meanwhile, you must meet Aubry where he is. Accept that he's struggling. Don't tell him you understand: you can't, but you can support him."

Palms damp, Estelle laced her fingers together and nodded. "I will do as you say. C-Can I call on you?"

"Absolutely, and I will stop by on occasion. When we make God part of the problem, He will provide the solution."

Estelle sighed. She wanted to send a letter that claimed she'd stand by him, but what if she changed her mind after mailing the missive?

"Captain DeLuca, you've got mail."

Aubry pushed himself up in the bed as Mitch strode toward him.

The orderly waved the envelope, then held it to his nose and sniffed loudly. "Smells like a good one. From that girl of yours, I'd say."

"How do you know it's not from my mother?" Pulse racing, Aubry reached out to snatch the missive, but Mitch held it aloft. Aubry pasted a mock frown on his face. "I'm going to report you for antagonizing the patients. You'll be reduced to swabbing floors." He was used to Mitch's teasing, but he wouldn't let the man know he was terrified about what was in the letter.

"Ha! It will be your word against mine." Mitch grinned and dropped the envelope onto Aubry's lap, then perched on the edge of the bed. He crossed his arms. "Ready when you are."

Aubry's eyebrow shot up. "This is personal."

"And I'm a personal friend, so here I sit."

"Personal friend, right."

"Hey, we've been through a lot."

"No, I've been through a lot with *you.*" Aubry chuckled. "First, you badger me to death at the convalescent hospital, then you managed to get yourself assigned as my escort on the flight to the States, and now you're here at Walter Reed."

Holding up his hands as if in surrender, Mitch shook his head. "I had nothing to do with it. I collected enough points to rotate stateside. Can I help it if they think I'm worthy of a job at the military's leading medical facility?"

"Right. That's what happened. You're a man of secrets. I wouldn't be surprised to discover you're Eisenhower's nephew."

Mitch guffawed. "Wouldn't that be something? Me, an Eisenhower." He flicked his fingers at the envelope. "Enough stalling. Read your letter."

"But—"

"All kidding aside, I want to be here for you. It's her first letter after getting the Dear Jane you insisted on sending, even though I cautioned against doing that."

"Thank you, Dr. Freud." Sarcasm dripped from Aubry's words. "Fine." He picked up the letter and tore open the flap.

"Careful, old man."

"Right." Mouth dry, Aubry slipped out the single sheet of light-blue paper and unfolded it. Surely, Estelle wouldn't have perfumed the envelope if she was leaving him as he suggested. Did he want her to stay with him? His gaze raced down the page, and the tightness in his chest eased. He cleared his throat.

"Dearest Aubry,

It was wonderful to hear from you after receiving the telegram about your being wounded. There was no information as to the extent of your injuries, and for many days, your mother and I didn't know how you fared. You'd think the government would spare no expense in telling family members about their loved ones. It was as if the War Information Office was paying by the word."

Mitch laughed. "She's a pistol."

"You have no idea."

"I'm beginning to get one. Now, continue."

"Before I go any further in the letter, I want you to know that I'm staying. You can push me away, but I'm not going anywhere. I'm not a fair-weather friend. I thought you knew me better than that.

"I was stunned to hear that you are nearby, well, near enough, and I wanted to come for a visit, but when I called to make arrangements, I was told I wasn't allowed to come. So, we're stuck with writing letters for now, but know that I would be by your side if I could be. I hope they're treating you well, and that you're behaving. Your mother says you've never been a good patient.

"Work is going well and very busy. Despite working long days, people need to escape the many reminders of war, so our patrons visit often and check out many books. Interestingly, the works of Raymond Chandler, Dashiell Hammett, and Agatha Christie are very popular. As you know, my preferences lie with the classics, but perhaps we can try one of Miss Christie's when you come home.

"Out of room, so I must close, but I am praying for you.

Your girl,

Estelle"

"She's a keeper, DeLuca." Mitch stood and poked Aubry's chest. "I'm pleased she's sticking by you. Not all the guys have that." He sighed. "Relationships are the biggest casualty of war, but nobody admits it."

Aubry jammed the letter into the envelope. "I should have been more specific about my injuries. She can't possibly be willing to stand by a man who can barely see. I need to write her again, tell her what's wrong with me. Once she hears, she'll be on her way."

"You're not giving her much credit, old man, but I do agree that giving her the truth of the situation is a good idea. That way she won't be shocked when she finally sees you. But be gentle, Captain. Before you write, you need to decide if you're going to hang on to your bitterness or if you're willing to accept what's happened. Dealing with your injury is one thing, but no woman should be subjected to a daily barrage of anger for the rest of her life." He turned on his heel and headed out the door.

Face hot, Aubry closed his eyes and held the fragrant envelope up to his nose. Mitch never pulled his punches, but he never spoke out of meanness. And if he wasn't a fellow wounded veteran, Aubry would have told him what he could do with his opinion, even if the orderly was right in his assessment.

Chapter Six

Conversation swirled around Aubry in the dormitory-style hospital room. Two weeks had passed since receiving Estelle's letter, claiming she'd be waiting for him when he got home. Two weeks during which he'd had too much time to think. Too much time to stare at the walls, willing his vision to improve. Too much time to yell at God and ask Him why He'd allowed his injuries. No answer had been forthcoming.

Mitch came by whenever he was on shift, ostensibly to check on Aubry's progress, but in reality, to offer encouragement and advice. Unwanted advice. His lips twisted. Like no one he'd ever known, the man was an intriguing combination of sensitivity and candor. A strong faith in God influenced his every word and action. Like the doctor at the evac hospital the man had missed his calling and should be a preacher. His constant cheerfulness—no, Mitch said it was joy—was annoying, yet Aubry looked forward to his visits and would miss the man more than he'd like to concede.

Three more long missives had come from Estelle, chatty with news from home, but no mention or questions about his injuries. Odd, in one sense. She was one of the most curious people he'd ever met, probably why she was a librarian. Her idea of a good time was to spend hours researching a topic.

She was also gracious and kind, two of the traits that grabbed him when they met. Thinking he'd be upset with talk of his wounds, she'd focused on small talk. Did he appreciate that or wish she'd probed the topic with her usual tenacity? He raked his fingers through his hair and sighed. Communication between the two of them didn't used to be this hard, but the war had changed everything.

Laughter broke through the murmuring, and he turned to see what caused the merriment. Three guys from the navy, who'd been admitted three days ago, were hunched over an issue of *Yank* magazine. One of the men said something, and the other two guffawed. A nurse hurried over and cautioned them to be quiet as she wagged her finger at them, her reprimand softened by the smile on her face.

Aubry smirked. At least the men had the grace to look abashed for making such a racket. They were in a hospital, not a nightclub. Granted, the patients here were well on their way to recovery, but that didn't mean that a little peace and quiet wasn't necessary.

"Captain DeLuca?"

"Yes?" Aubry hadn't noticed the approaching orderly. "What is it?"

The burly man held out a slip of paper. "Your hospital discharge papers, sir. A nurse will be in shortly with your duffel bag and travel orders."

"Discharge?"

"Yes, sir. You'll be transported to Fort George G. Meade, where they'll process you out, then you can make your way home, which I understand isn't too far." The orderly beamed. "You made it, sir. You made it through. Congratulations."

"Thanks," Aubry growled as he snatched the page from the man's hand. "How soon before the nurse arrives?" He'd had enough of doctors, nurses, and do-gooders. Enough of the acrid smell of disinfectant. The sooner he could leave, the better.

"Now, that's no way to treat the bearer of good news."

Aubry lifted his head. Where had Mitch come from? With his skill of seeming to appear out of nowhere, the man should have been in the Office of Strategic Services. "I simply asked a question."

"Right. I'll take it from here, Ivan."

"Yes, sir." The orderly dipped his head toward Aubry, then turned on his heel and walked away.

"No lectures, please." Aubry scowled. "I'm tired of being told what to do."

"For a man who's one step closer to home, you're in a foul mood." Mitch sat on the edge of the bed. "Nervous about the bus ride or cranky for no apparent reason?"

A sigh bubbled up in Aubry's chest, but he clamped his lips together and shrugged.

"Okay, suit yourself." Mitch rose and extended his arm. "Best of luck, Captain. I'll be praying for you."

Letting the sigh escape, Aubry shook his hand, shoulders slumping. "Thanks. I'll take all the prayers I can get. I'm not sure God is listening to me at the moment."

"He is, but you know that." Mitch grinned. "And you asked me not to lecture you."

Aubry snorted a laugh. "And you've obeyed my requests every time." He sobered up, then brought his hand to his forehead in a crisp salute. "Thank you for being a friend, Mitch. I won't forget you."

"Nor I, you." Mitch returned the salute, then glanced toward the doorway where a tall, brunette nurse entered, carrying a canvas bag. "Looks like your personal stuff has arrived, so I'll let you get to it. Take care."

"You, too." He swallowed the lump that had formed in his throat and forced his lips into a smile. "Now, go annoy one of the other patients."

With a guffaw, Mitch clapped Aubry on the back and nodded. "Don't mind if I do." He gestured for the nurse to come to the bed, then strolled down the aisle of beds to the far end of the room.

Aubry watched his friend stop beside one of the patients. Would he ever find the joy Mitch promised could be had?

Rumbling through the gate at Fort Meade, the bus bucked as the driver ground the vehicle's gears. Aubry flinched at the sound. Had they left the transmission on the road? He peered out the grimy window, then adjusted the patch over his left eye and grimaced. The vision in his uncovered eye remained cloudy. What did he think he was going to see?

Brakes squealing, the bus stopped in front of an ugly brick building. Most of the men jumped up and jostled each other in their eagerness to disembark, but Aubry remained in his seat. He hadn't sent his mother or Estelle a cable, so his appearance would be a surprise, perhaps a shock. Maybe he'd find some place to crash and put off going home.

"Last stop, Captain." The driver turned to look at Aubry. "I gotta take this old girl to the motor pool."

Aubry glanced around. He was alone. "Sorry." He gripped his duffel bag and climbed to his feet, then trudged off the bus. At the bottom of the steps, he hesitated. He shielded his eye from the glare of the afternoon sun. The air was thick with humidity, and sweat pooled under his arms. Where to? His fellow riders were barreling through the door of the administration building, which meant at least an hour of waiting for his turn to be processed out.

"If you're lookin' for something to do, the USO club is in the next building over." The driver called through the open window. "Lots of pretty girls and great food. You can get something to eat, turn the rug with one of them gals, or just talk—your choice. You can also do one of them fancy recordings to send to your family."

"Thanks." Aubry slung the bag over his shoulder and sauntered in the direction the man had indicated. His ears pricked up at the sound of Benny Goodman's signature clarinet. He increased his pace, then paused in front of yet another unattractive structure. Laughter and voices mingled with the music, giving the place a cocktail party atmosphere, although he'd heard the USO didn't serve alcohol, and the girls had strict rules governing their behavior. They'd be nice to him because they had to. It was their job to cheer up the soldiers.

Frowning, he turned away.

"Hey, don't leave. The excitement's just getting started."

Aubry whirled.

A petite blonde, wearing a pink-and-white, polka-dotted dress and white pumps, stood at the door, hand on her hip. "Cook just made a fresh pot of coffee, and we've got more sandwiches than we know what to do with. Help us out."

"I'm not hungry."

"You're just saying that because you think it's army food and won't be very good, but you've got it all wrong. Cook is from one of the big-time restaurants in Washington and works the kitchen during the day. The food's delish." She motioned toward the inside of the building. "You won't regret it. I promise you."

"I said I'm not hungry," Aubry snarled. "I don't need anything to eat, and I certainly don't need your pity, so leave me alone."

Her eyes widened, and she jerked back as if slapped. A split second passed, then her smile returned, albeit a bit forced. "As you wish, but we're here if you change your mind." She pivoted and disappeared inside.

Aubry's stomach hollowed. He should rush into the building, find the woman, and apologize. He'd been a brute, and she didn't deserve the treatment. His feet wouldn't move, as if they were nailed to the road, and his heart threatened to jump from his chest. His vision, what little he had, narrowed, and dizziness swept over him, then the world went black.

CHAPTER SEVEN

Estelle pressed a hand against her stomach, but her insides continued to quiver as if a flock of hummingbirds was trapped. Mouth dry, she swallowed, then licked her lips. Her breath came in short bursts. She hadn't been this nervous since...well, never. She took a final look at her reflection, then grabbed her pocketbook and fled the bedroom.

Mrs. Feeney had visited again last night. She'd heard Aubry was home and came over to offer encouragement and advice. Her words had been a balm to Estelle's ravaged soul, and she'd felt prepared by the time the elderly woman left, but this morning doubts and confusion returned.

"Lord, help me meet Aubry where he is, like Mrs. Feeney said. Guide me and keep me from saying or doing anything insensitive. Or stupid."

"What's that, dear?" Estelle's mother's voice floated down the hall from the kitchen. "I didn't hear you."

"Nothing, Mother." Estelle's grip on her purse tightened. "I'm headed out to visit Aubry."

Footsteps sounded, then her mother appeared, her brow wrinkled. She wiped her hands on her apron, not quite removing the coating of flour on her skin. "Will you be all right? Do you want company?"

"I'm fine. Besides, Mrs. DeLuca will be there. Too many folks would be overwhelming."

"True." She brightened, then kissed Estelle's cheek. "I hope things go well."

The hummingbirds took flight again, and Estelle gulped. "I'm sure they will. I'll be back in time for lunch. Mrs. Feeney suggested that I make this first visit short."

"Probably a good idea."

Estelle cocked her head. "Do you mind if I use the car? I've managed to miss the bus, and the next one won't come for a while."

"Absolutely, dear. I've hardly used any gas this week and have no plans to go out until church on Sunday."

"Thanks, Mother. You're the best."

"And you're trying to butter me up." Estelle's mother chuckled. "But you already got what you want."

"It never hurts to build up points." Estelle smirked. "At least that's what Daddy tells me."

Her mother pinked and waved one hand in a dismissive gesture. "Your father is a piece of work."

With a giggle, Estelle nodded. "See you later." Shaking her head, she hurried to the garage. Married nearly thirty years, yet her mother had blushed like a schoolgirl at the mention of Estelle's father and his teasing ways. Her parents weren't overly demonstrative with their love, but she knew they cared deeply for each other. The occasional touch or glance said it all, but she'd never seen her mother turn red.

She slid into the driver's seat and turned the key. The engine roared to life, and she pulled the dark green Ford out of the garage and onto the street. Would she and Aubry find a love like her parents had? Would she flush at the thought of him when they were old and gray? Not that her mother and father were *that* old. Not like Mr. and Mrs. Feeney.

Guiding the vehicle down the road, her thoughts tumbled like a gymnast at the Olympics. What would it be like to spend the rest of her life with the same man? Did couples run out of things to say to each other? Her parents didn't seem to have that problem, but perhaps they were different than other folks. Did she care for Aubry enough to be with him for the next forty or fifty years? Maybe even more. Her friend's granny and grandpa were still going strong at ninety years old.

Too soon she was in front of the DeLuca's brick ranch-style home. Her palms were moist as she stopped the car. She raked her gaze over the manicured lawn and numerous flower gardens that dotted the landscape. Pink azalea bushes stood sentry on either side of the front door. An ancient maple tree cast its massive shadow over much of the driveway.

Pulse thrumming, she climbed out of the car. A warm breeze that promised another scorching day lifted her hair. She straightened her shoulders. *Meet him where he is.* Mrs. Feeney's words floated in Estelle's head.

"You're being ridiculous, girl. He's the same man he was." She marched up to the door, raised her hand, and knocked. What if he wasn't the same man?

The door swung open, and Mrs. DeLuca beamed at her, then pulled her into a tight, but brief, hug. "You came."

"Of course." Estelle squeezed the woman's shoulder, then leaned close. "How is he?"

"Anxious to see you," Mrs. DeLuca whispered. "But loathe to admit it." She gave Estelle a small push. "He's in the living room. I'll be in with some iced tea shortly."

A tight grip on her purse and her emotions, Estelle tramped through the corridor until she reached the doorway.

Aubry rose from the overstuffed couch, his hands clasped in front of him. He wore a pair of tan slacks and a light-blue cotton shirt buttoned to the neck. His short hair was slicked down, and his olive skin, normally deeply tanned by this time of year, was pale and in sharp contrast to his dark, closely cropped beard. His right eye held a distant gaze, and a black patch was strapped over his left eye, giving him a piratical air.

Her breath caught. Aubry's mother hadn't said anything about him losing an eye. Her hand flew to her throat, and she blinked away the tears that threatened to fall. Despite the covering over his eye, he was as handsome as she remembered. More so with the angular planes of his face sharp from weight loss. A scar puckered his forehead above the patch but only served to enhance his rugged good looks.

His tentative smile turned into a scowl, and she rushed toward him. "I'm sorry, Aubry. I'm so overwhelmed that you're home." She wrapped her arms around his lean body and tucked her head under his chin. Would he think her too forward? Their relationship had been close before he left, but they'd kept physical contact to a minimum.

Rigid, he stood with his arms at his sides. His heart thumped against her, matching her own frantic rhythm. Was he as nervous as she was? Smiling, she snuggled closer. "I've missed you."

A sigh ruffled her hair, and his arms enveloped her.

Footsteps approached, and they sprang apart, her face burning as if she'd stood hovered over a campfire. A moment later, Mrs. DeLuca appeared caring a tray topped with a green porcelain pitcher and two glasses, as well as a plate of cookies. She put the tray on the coffee table. "Don't leave your guest standing, dear."

Face as red as Estelle's felt, Aubry motioned to the couch, and she sank onto the cushion, then he dropped beside her. What did his mother think of her, clinging to her son?

Aware of Estelle's lithe form but unable to see her from his peripheral vision because of his patch, Aubry clenched his hands into fists. Even if he turned toward her, sight from his right eye was still poor, and she was little more than a blur. Would he ever be able to gaze at her with clarity? See the outline of her porcelain face? The sparkle in her eyes or the shimmer of her cinnamon-colored hair?

She'd trembled in his arms. Was she frightened or nervous? Or was her shiver out of pity? Why had she come? A desire to see him or obligation?

His mother bent and kissed his cheek. "I'll be in the kitchen, so holler if you need anything else." As usual, her voice was overly loud as if he were deaf instead of blind. He'd given up reminding her he could hear.

He settled back on the cushions and crossed his legs while Estelle poured their drinks. As she handed him his glass, her scent wafted over him. The crisp aroma of soap mingled with the sweet fragrance of flowers, lilacs if he remembered correctly. His stomach flipped, and his grasp tightened on the glass. Sipping his tea, for something to do, he could hear his mother puttering in the other room. She made enough noise to remind them of her presence, but not too much to be intrusive. As if they needed a chaperone at their ages.

"I suppose—"

"How—"

They laughed, and he motioned for her to speak. "Ladies, first."

She licked her lips, then cleared her throat. "How are you settling in? It must feel strange to be home: good, but strange."

"Both of those, yes." He rubbed his hands on his slacks. "Frankly, I'm having trouble sleeping. You would think now that I'm reclining on a mattress instead of the ground, I'd sleep like a baby."

"I'm not sure who thought of that saying." She giggled. "Babies wake up constantly."

He chuckled. "Then it fits. With any luck, the restlessness will pass."

"It's too quiet, isn't it?"

"That's part of the problem." He frowned. "Are you asking me what it was like? Do you want to know?" He set down his glass with a thump, then crossed his arms.

"Only if you want to tell me, but that's not why I'm here. I just want to be with you, see you, know that you're home. We used to be comfortable being quiet, sitting together without talking. Has that changed?"

"I-I don't know."

"Okay." She sipped her tea. "I can tell you about what's happened in town since you left. Would you like that? Or would you like me to leave? Have I stayed too long?"

"No! I mean, uh, no." He swallowed. "I'd like you to stay." He lowered his voice. "As uncomfortable as this is, it's better than being alone with my mother. She's alternately chipper or mournful."

"She's doing the best she can." Estelle's tone held a slight rebuke. "Your mother has been alone for nearly three years wondering if she was going to lose you, too."

His breath whooshed out as if punched in the gut. "I didn't think of that. She always seemed so, I don't know, together, after Dad died. I hadn't thought of how my death or injury would affect her."

Her hand rested on his thigh for a quick moment, then as if she realized how intimate the gesture was, yanked it away. "You can't expect everything to go back to normal right away. Like it or not, you're still healing, and it's going to take a while. Your mother is thrilled to have you home, and her behavior is going to be somewhat erratic while she adjusts. Give each other some grace."

He cocked his head and studied her, as best he could, considering his clouded vision. Apparently, he wasn't the only one who'd grown up over the last two and a half years. "When did you get to be so wise?"

Her face flushed with a lovely pink tinge, and she shrugged. "I can't imagine what you experienced, but to be honest, life here at home hasn't been all sunshine and rainbows. We lived through difficulties, shortages, and fear."

"Fear? What did you have to be afraid of?" He winced at the sarcasm in his voice. "I mean, you were safe and secure here in the States."

"We know that now, but we've been watching for enemy airplanes and listening to reports, waiting to be attacked just like Pearl

Harbor. Laurel is only twenty miles from DC, the perfect location for the Germans to bomb." She hunched into herself. "And then there was the fear of the next casualty report, the next telegram. To hear who we'd lost. Was our life as terrifying as yours? No. But as scary and distressing? Yes."

"I'm sorry. I didn't—"

"It's me who should be sorry." She jumped up, her face rosy. "What a tirade. I should go. I can't believe I—"

He tugged her hand and pulled her down on the couch. "It's okay. We're trying to figure this out." He barked a harsh laugh. "You remind me of Mitch. One of the orderlies. He never pulled any punches, either. He'd love you."

Estelle had changed. Still gracious and warm, but with more steel in her backbone. In the few weeks they'd known each other before he was drafted, she often acquiesced to his thoughts and opinions. Apparently, she'd had time to form her own while he was gone. Getting reacquainted might not be as seamless as he'd anticipated.

CHAPTER EIGHT

Noises continued to come from the kitchen as Estelle rested her hand in Aubry's palm, the same but different. His long, tapered fingers were the same shape, and his hand still engulfed her smaller one, but there were scars and callouses that hadn't previously existed. Hard places that hadn't been there, kind of like this new Aubry.

She saw glimmers of the man he was, but there was a darkness about him that seemed to hover like the beginnings of a summer storm when pewter-colored clouds held the promise of rain, perhaps even a deluge. Was thunder and lightning on its way between them?

Mrs. Feeney's wise words intruded: *Meet him where he is,* and the tension seeped from Estelle's shoulders. She sagged against the cushion and squeezed Aubry's hand. "We used to read aloud to each other. Would you like that?" She gestured toward her pocketbook. "I brought your favorite, *Riders of the Purple Sage.*"

"We could do that." He shrugged, and his tone was dull. "I can't reciprocate at this point. You'll have to do all the reading."

Her stomach clenched. Was apathy worse than anger? Mrs. Feeney said he might suffer from outbursts of rage, sometimes for no apparent reason. But Aubry seemed defeated rather than upset. How could she draw him out? She bent and pulled out the book, then laid it in her lap. "I don't mind, as long as you don't get sick of hearing me."

"I can't imagine that happening. The sweet, light voice of a woman will be a nice change."

She shot him a wry smile. "Any woman?"

"Well...I meant—"

"Relax. I was teasing." She swallowed a sigh. They had a long road ahead of them. Today was more awkward than their first date. She cleared her throat and opened the book, smoothing the pages with tentative fingers. She began to read, "A sharp clip-clop of iron-shod hoofs deadened and died away."

"A book saved my life."

"What?" Estelle's eyes widened, and her grip tightened on the book. "How?"

Another shrug. "Fortunately, I wasn't carrying one of those Armed Services Editions. Too thin and flimsy. I don't think one of them would have done the job."

Nibbling the inside of her cheek, Estelle froze. According to Mrs. Feeney, he would say what he wanted when he wanted to say it. Pushing him or asking questions wouldn't help and might upset him.

"Yeah, those ASE books are good. I read a bunch of them. They helped pass the time in between the fighting. We'd swap them among ourselves and other units. A good idea, those books. Sometimes, I could actually escape from reality."

Estelle nodded, afraid to say anything and break his ruminations.

"Did you know they printed over a thousand titles? That's what one of the guys told me. Not sure how true it is. Do you know?" He sounded like a little boy, innocent and inquisitive.

"No, I'm sorry, I don't. But we could find out. They might know at the library." Her mouth dry, she eyed her glass of iced tea. Would he ever get back to what happened to save his life? Had he really almost died? Her heart pounded. How could he be so nonchalant?

"Good idea." He leaned back against the cushion and closed his eyes, the black patch stark against his skin. "Go ahead and keep reading."

"Are you tired? Have I worn out my welcome?"

"Hardly."

"Okay." She fidgeted on the seat as she studied him. *Dear Lord, thank You for performing a miracle and saving him. Forgive me for my harsh words to him about how we suffered at home. Our lives were easy compared to the awfulness he experienced, the horror of killing and waiting to be killed.* Tears pricked the backs of her eyes, and a lump formed in her throat.

"Hey, you all right?" His eye flew open, and he sat up. Leaning toward her, he peered at her face. "I may not be able to see too well, but I can tell you're upset. What's wrong? What'd I say?"

"Nothing."

"Liar." He grinned, taking the sting from the word. "Tell me."

"A book saved your life, which meant I almost lost you. I was thanking God for the miracle."

He frowned. "Yeah, I still can't decide if that's a good thing."

Her jaw dropped. "How can you say that?"

"Easy." He sliced the air with one hand and glared at her. "I don't want to talk about it. You wouldn't understand. Read."

Silence stretched between them as she returned his look. He was right. She didn't understand, but that didn't mean they should sweep the topic under the rug. She might have to meet him where he was, but she deserved the same treatment, didn't she? "You're right, and I don't claim to, but I'll listen if you ever do want to discuss it."

His gaze shifted, then he closed his eyes again and resumed his position against the back of the couch, fingers laced together.

"If you tell me what book it is, I'll check it out of the library."

He bolted upright. "What? Why?"

She bit the inside of her cheek. Would he appreciate her attempt at humor? "Well, if it saved your life, I'm assuming it is, uh, damaged, and you didn't get to finish it."

His mouth formed a perfect O, and his eye was wide, filled with an emotion she couldn't determine. Did he think she was belittling the event? Would he throw her out of the house? Time stood still as she held her breath.

Then his lips twitched, and he guffawed for a long moment. "Aren't you the sassy one?"

A giggle bubbled up inside her, then escaped. He wasn't angry. But what would happen next time?

A pan crashed in the kitchen, and Aubry's mother called out, "Sorry. A bit fumbly today."

Aubry blinked as Estelle's smile faltered. The moment was broken, and he crossed his arms. "Please keep reading."

A nod, then she licked her lips. Her very kissable lips. She'd done that several times since arriving. A nervous habit? Did he make her skittish? Was she afraid of him? What had she been told to expect?

He sighed and dropped his chin to his chest. Who knew coming home would be so hard?

"Lie back again." She gently pushed him against the cushion. "I'll pick up where I left off."

His eyes fluttered, then closed. Her voice washed over him, rising and falling with the cadence of the story. Then her words faded as his mind took him back to the beach in France. The heat of the desert of the Old West transformed into the damp and frigid coast of *La Manche,* the *sleeve,* as the French called the English Channel. Shells fell from the sky, some bombarding the soldiers as they tumbled out of the tank landing ships known as LSTs into the rough seas, many exploding as they hit the ground. He'd already made it to shore, and the sand shifted under his feet as he struggled to find purchase. Comrades fell beside him, sometimes silently, others moaning in agony as they writhed on the ground.

By the end of the day, the weather had turned fair, almost balmy, but bad weather from the previous day had continued through the morning of the invasion, making it seem as if heaven mourned with them. He later discovered the Germans had pulled back, believing the weather was too poor for the Allies to attack. A blessing, to be sure, but they'd still lost too many men. *He'd* lost too many men. Men he'd trained, then led straight into the teeth of the monster. Men who'd become friends, some closer than others.

His eyes—no, correction—his one eye, burned, the other useless, but no tears emerged. Only a fierce rage that he needed to keep hidden deep in the recesses of his being. He couldn't let it out.

Estelle's voice intruded, and the darkness receded. She was a good woman. Different than he remembered. Yet in some ways, the same. She'd taken a chance by teasing him about the book that had taken the bullet for him. Should he tell her the details? Did he want to see the shock and horror on her face as she realized how close he came to dying? Did he want her to hurt, to feel the terror that had coursed through him when he realized he'd cheated death?

She'd called it a miracle. Had God intervened, or was it luck of the draw? As a believer, he wasn't supposed to believe in luck. But had God been at Normandy that day? Seen the carnage? If He had been present, would fewer men have died? Had He sent the weather to ensure

Allied victory? Why had He allowed Hitler to get into power in the first place?

He hadn't asked his mother about his friends from town. How many of them remained? Were there others who'd been shipped home, broken, or maimed? Who had fallen, never to return? Could he live here knowing he'd never see some of those boys again? Knowing they were forever gone? What would life be like moving forward?

Mitch's face appeared in his mind, the orderly's crooked grin and twinkling eyes bringing a smile. If anyone had a right to be bitter, it was Mitch, but he'd accepted his lot and the loss of his leg with sardonic grace. "Take one day at a time, Aubry," he'd said a couple of days before Aubry had been discharged. "Life on earth is hard. We shouldn't be surprised when terrible things happen to us, but God is bigger than this war. He's in charge. Never forget that."

He didn't forget, but he was struggling to believe it. How can a benevolent God allow a war that killed millions of people? Allow him to lose his sight? Would he ever regain his vision well enough to take a job? How could he provide for a family if he couldn't see? No one in their right mind would hire a blindman. Would he be relegated to spending the rest of his life being cared for by his mother? No woman would marry a man who couldn't see. Estelle would wake up one day soon and realize that. Perhaps he should let her down now and walk away. It would be best for both of them.

It might be best, but it would be the hardest thing he ever did, even compared to war.

CHAPTER NINE

A knock sounded at the front door, and Aubry stiffened. Who was coming to visit? No one he wanted to see, he could bet on that. He clenched his fists. He'd have to pass the door to get to his room upstairs, and with his bum leg, he'd never make it before his mother answered the knock. His heart pounded, and he turned toward Estelle.

She'd risen. Was she going to leave him stranded to deal with whoever had shown up?

"Stay put." Estelle skirted the coffee table. "I'll get it, Mrs. DeLuca."

"Thank you, dear," Aubry's mother's muffled voice came from the kitchen.

"I don't—"

"Don't worry." She smiled and left the room.

He knotted his fingers together. Easy for her to say. She didn't have to worry about people gawking at her, asking stupid questions, probing for information that was none of their business. Did she know he had no interest in entertaining friends? He'd barely tolerated the thought of her visit, but things had turned out okay.

Nausea swept over him, and he swallowed. Sweat dotted his forehead, and he pulled out his handkerchief to blot away the moisture. Being in a foxhole was easier than this.

A deep voice rumbled in the foyer, followed by Estelle's soft, musical tones. Then footsteps, the heavy tread of a large man followed by the *tap tap* of Estelle's high-heeled shoes.

Gritting his teeth, he struggled to stand. He'd greet whoever it was on his feet, straight and tall, not like the invalid they thought him to be.

Mitch strode through the doorway, enveloped Aubry in a tight hug, then released him and clapped him on the shoulder. "Look at you, old man."

Aubry's legs nearly buckled, and he locked his knees to keep from keeling over. His throat thickened at the sight of his friend. Speechless, he gawked at Mitch. He should have recognized the sound the man's rolling gait.

"I've knocked the words right out of you." Mitch rocked on his heels and grinned at Estelle. "I usually can't get him to shut up."

She giggled. "That's always been my problem, too." She walked to Aubry and kissed his cheek. "I'll leave you two to visit but will be back after work tomorrow, if you're up for it." She shook Mitch's hand and said, "Nice to meet you," then strolled out the door.

Aubry's pulse raced as the lasting scent of soap and lilacs enveloped him. His cheek tingled where her lips had pressed against the skin. His mother hurried into the room, diverting his attention.

She carried a glass of iced tea and smiled so broadly her eyes nearly closed. "Are you one of Aubry's friends from the army?"

"No, ma'am. I'm Mitch Watkins, and we met at the hospital." He took the drink. "I was stationed as an orderly at the convalescent hospital, then followed him to Walter Reed. I've got a few days off and thought I'd see how this lout is settling in."

"Wonderful. I'll leave you boys to visiting." She wagged her finger at him. "Plan to stay for lunch and dinner."

"I don't want to put you out."

Aubry shook his head. "It's no use to turn down the invitation. She'll badger you until she gets a yes. I'm glad for her to have someone else to fuss over."

"Then I accept."

"Excellent." She beamed at Mitch. "Now, you boys have fun, and I'll be out front in the garden." With a wave, she walked out.

"I can't believe you're here." Aubry motioned to the chair, then returned to his seat on the couch. "Did you have absolutely no other possibility of something to do today?"

"Funny." Mitch smirked. "Actually, I'm on an errand for the hospital, and I realized you were on the way, so I asked permission to make a detour."

"And you don't have to be back tonight?"

"Nope."

"Is this a pity visit, or do the docs expect a report?" Aubry was unsuccessful in keeping the edge out of his voice, so he forced a smile.

"Neither." Mitch swatted Aubry's leg. "I thought we were friends, old man. Am I wrong?"

"No. I'm sorry. I don't—"

"Don't apologize. I get it. I've been where you are. You're being smothered by a well-intentioned mother, and still not sure where you stand with your girl. If you've been to town, you've been stared at, whispered about, or ignored. How am I doing so far?"

The tightness in Aubry's chest dissipated, and a sigh seeped out. "You do know."

"Yep." Sadness flitted across Mitch's face. "Most people mean well, but they don't know how to act, so..." He spread his hands and shrugged. "How are the nightmares? Any better?"

"Some." Aubry frowned. "But what's odd is that my mind will wander in the middle of a conversation. Some word or smell will trigger a thought, and the next thing I know I'm on the beach. It happened while Estelle was reading to me. She was...disconcerted."

"She seems like a good gal. We only had a few minutes at the door, but she's nice. Seems stable, not flighty."

"You could tell all that?" Aubry narrowed his eyes. "Is that your professional opinion?"

"Hardly, but I'm a decent judge of character." Mitch leaned back in the chair. "She looked me in the eye and didn't yammer or try to tell me how great you're doing as if she had something to prove. And I saw how she looked at you."

"With pity?"

"Come off it, old man. You're the only one who's subjected yourself to pity. People care about you. You have to let them show it."

"It-it's difficult."

"Probably one of the hardest things you'll ever do." Mitch nodded. "You're a man who stands on his own two feet. You led men into battle, and now you have to let others take care of you. It's awful. But little by little, you'll heal, physically and emotionally; that one takes the longest, by the way." He raked his fingers through his short hair, causing it to spike in several places. "Give it time. Give *her* time."

Aubry's eyebrow shot up. "I—"

"Listen, you were only getting to know each other when you were called up. You've been separated for more than two years. You can't expect to pick up where you left off. Unfortunately, my friend, you have to start over. Don't rush things. You have plenty of time to woo her."

"Actually, I've been thinking about breaking it off."

"Really?" Mitch tilted his head. "Have your feelings for her changed?"

"She doesn't need to be trapped in a marriage with...me. Wouldn't be fair."

"Why not?" Mitch's lips thinned. "Just because you've got a few scars? Can't see as well as you used to? How about if you let her make that decision."

"She—"

"You think my wife is trapped? Stuck with a cripple because I lost a leg?"

"No, that's different."

Mitch crossed his arms. "I beg to differ. You are the same man you were in 1941, albeit a little more beat up, unless you let bitterness and anger take root. Be yourself. Be the man she fell in love with. You can't go wrong."

"Yeah, I can."

Chapter Ten

Seated behind the mammoth wooden circulation desk, Estelle smiled as a young woman entered the library holding the hand of a towheaded little boy. Five or six years old, the child skipped beside her, his neck swiveling as he took in the activity. His eyes sparkled. "Come on, Mama, we've got to find the book. You promised." His strident voice broke the silence.

"Shh." The woman sent Estelle an apologetic look. "We must keep our voice down."

"It's exciting to visit the library, isn't it?" Estelle beckoned the youngster. "There are so many adventures to be had. It's my favorite place to be."

He raced forward with a grin. "That's what Mama said! Do you know her?"

"No. How about if you introduce us."

"Okay. This is my mama." His brow wrinkled. "Wait, what's your name?"

"Miss Johnson."

"Mama, this is Miss Johnson."

The young woman gazed at her son with love, then back at Estelle. "It's lovely to meet you. I'm Martha Holt, and this is Billy."

"I haven't seen you before today. I'd remember a smart boy like you." Estelle cocked her head. "Is this your first time to visit the library, Billy?"

"Yes, we just moved here. Daddy got a job with the army, so Mama and me are living with Grandma. She smells nice, like flowers."

Billy's mother shrugged, apparently used to her son's opinions, but a mixture of fear and sadness lurked in her eyes. Daddy's "job" was no doubt somewhere overseas fighting the enemy.

Estelle patted Billy's hand. "What book can I help you find?"

"*Curious George*. Do you have that?"

"Let's find out, shall we?" She poked her head into the office. "I'll be away from the desk for a moment, Mrs. Ryskamp. We have a new patron eager to avail himself of adventures."

"So I heard." Her boss snickered. "Let's not keep him waiting."

Rounding the desk, Estelle motioned toward the children's section. "Welcome to Laurel and the library. We offer lots of activities for kids, so I hope to see the two of you again."

Relief eased the lines on Martha's face, and she nodded.

With a flourish, Estelle pulled *Curious George* from the shelf and handed it to Billy. "Your wish is my command, sir. Enjoy!"

74

He cradled the book against his chest and beamed at her. "Thank you, Miss Johnson. You're the best. And you smell nice, too."

"Why, thank you." Estelle ruffled his hair, then squeezed Martha's shoulder. "I must go back to the desk, but come see me if you need more assistance." She chuckled to herself as she threaded her way through the shelves. Martha had her hands full with the youngster, that was certain.

Aubry's image as a little boy pushed its way into her mind. He hadn't been fair and blond like this child, but he did have the chubby cheeks of this lad. The photos she'd viewed with his mother, while they'd awaited news, showed an Aubry who looked out at the world as a grand adventure, eyes sparkling. Was that person still inside?

He'd been home for ten days and seemed less brittle each time she visited. Their routine of tea with his mother, then reading a couple of chapters created a sense of normalcy. She refrained from asking any questions that weren't related to the book. She desperately wanted to delve deeper into his life, to know what had happened during the years he was gone, but she knew better than to inquire. He'd tell her if and when he was ready, but the waiting was hard. Would he ever share his experiences?

She patted her hair, then went to the card catalog to rifle through the fiction section. They finished the Zane Gray book yesterday, so she needed to find something else to read. Should she select another one of the author's many novels or find another writer? Was *White Fang* too serious? What about a mystery? Would Aubry enjoy solving a murder, or would the character's death be too close to reality?

At church on Sunday, Mrs. DeLuca shared that he suffered from nightmares. Not every night, but often enough that the older woman was concerned. Should Estelle suggest he talk to one of the doctors at Fort Meade, or would he think she was meddling in his affairs? She nibbled on her lower lip. There was still uncertainty between them, awkward at times, as they tried to navigate getting reacquainted.

"Well, I heard he hasn't been seen since he returned home. That poor mother of his has to wait on him hand and foot."

"Appalling."

Estelle's ears pricked up as the voices of Mrs. Corson and Mrs. Trowbridge, notorious for spreading tales, floated toward her from behind the shelves. Loathe to correct the women because of the condescension they would probably shower on her, she rose and straightened her spine.

"What makes *him* so special? He should be taking care of her now that he's back."

"But he's been injured, badly, from what I hear."

"At least he's alive. The Vincents' son died at Normandy, as did many others from town. He needs to buck up."

Buck up? Estelle cringed at the woman's callous comment. Who were they talking about? She peeked around the bookcase, but they weren't in sight. Where were they?

"But I heard his face is badly scarred. His appearance is so bad, he wears a patch."

Estelle gasped, then clapped a hand over her mouth. Tears sprang to her eyes. They were talking about Aubry. No, not talking about him. Gossiping. She gritted her teeth and marched to the end of the aisle. She turned the corner, and the women looked up, neither appearing embarrassed to be caught.

"Ladies, this is a library. I'll thank you to lower your voices." She glared at them. "And to refrain from talking about Aubry DeLuca. You don't know anything about him or what he's gone through. Have you been to visit? No. So you can't possibly know what he looks like or how he's feeling or what his mother is doing for him." Breathing hard, she stood with her hands on her hips. Her words hung in the air between them. She'd overstepped her bounds speaking to her elders in such a manner, but someone needed to do it. Would they insist she be fired?

Mrs. Corson pursed her lips, and Mrs. Trowbridge raised her chin. "How dare you talk to me like that—"

"It's no less than you deserve."

Estelle cringed as she whirled to find the subject of their conversation standing behind them.

Satisfaction filled Aubry as he scowled at the pair of biddies, their guilt at being caught evident in their stance. Oh, if only his vision were better so he could see their faces, but their body language was enough. He knew their kind. They might feel bad at the moment, but that wouldn't stop them from flapping their gums. Silly know-it-alls, the lot of them. Rich, bored, and arrogant, thinking they are better than everyone else. He clenched his fists. The urge to shout at them was strong. If they were anywhere else but a library, he might have.

He limped closer, his grip tight on his cane, his spine as straight as he could make it. He narrowed his eyes at the women and stifled a grin as they seemed to shrink before his eyes. Not as brave when the object of their scorn was standing in front of them. "Anything you'd like to say, ladies?"

Dressed in silk suits with matching hats perched on their coiffed, white hair, neither one spoke but continued to stare at him. Their remorse had apparently dissipated to be replaced by curiosity and scorn.

"Here to pick up the book we discussed, Aubry?" Estelle touched his arm. "If you follow me to the desk, I can check it out for you."

"I'm good." Aubry cocked his head. "Well, ladies?"

The taller of the two sniffed and drew her pocketbook up to her chest. "You obviously don't know who I am, young man, or you would not be so rude." The woman glowered at Estelle. "Nor would you. I'll be speaking to Mrs. Ryskamp, but not today. Come, Myrtle, we're leaving." She swept past Aubry, her friend scurrying to keep up. He didn't bother to watch them leave.

"Aubry, how long—"

"Long enough." His thigh throbbed, and he locked his knees to keep from tumbling to the floor. Perspiration pooled under his arms. "I hate people like that. Their own lives are so small that they poke their noses into other people's."

"Hate is a strong word."

"What's your point?" He spoke through gritted teeth. "It's how I feel. Does that offend your sensibilities?"

Estelle stepped back. "No. Are you trying to shock me?"

"Are you?"

"Stop being so adversarial. You're angry at them, but taking it out on me. I don't appreciate that."

The air came out of his lungs as if punched. She never would have spoken to him like that before he left. Direct. Candid. More proof of how she'd changed. His thigh quivered, and he swayed.

She wrapped her arm around his waist. "Sit down before you fall down. Please tell me you didn't walk the entire way from the house?"

"Okay, I won't tell you."

The fresh scent of her filled his nose. She'd swapped her usual lilac fragrance for rosewater. Lovely. He inhaled deeply. Just like the flower, she was soft and beautiful, but thorny, too.

Shaking her head, she said, "There's a chair near the desk."

They made their way to the front of the library, and he dropped onto the chair with a grunt. He laid the cane across his lap and crossed his arms. "I don't need you to come to my rescue. I can take care of myself."

Face red, she bent behind the circulation desk, then stood up and put a book on the gleaming surface. "Yes, you can. However, I was unaware of your presence. They were talking too loudly, and their topic was unacceptable. I might have been a bit...zealous in my reprimand, but—"

"You were angry."

"I don't like gossips." She tugged at her earlobe. "There wasn't a shred of truth in what they were saying."

"They're going to talk about you now, you know. Going to tattle to your boss, too. Sticking up for me might get you fired."

"I doubt it, but if that's what happens, so be it. I wouldn't change how I responded. They needed to be told."

"Their kind doesn't take kindly to that sort of behavior."

"Perhaps." She tapped the book with her index finger. "I thought we could try something different to read. *White Fang*. What do you think?"

"Changing the subject, are you?" Aubry's stomach hardened. She was coddling him. First, telling off the old crones, now picking out books as if he were incapable.

"You know I'm not some scrawny, eight-year-old kid who needs defending or waiting on."

"I didn't—"

He winced as he climbed to his feet. "How about if we pass on getting together tonight? I'd like to be alone." Without waiting for a response, he turned and stalked to the door willing his leg to hold him upright.

Chapter Eleven

A light breeze ruffled Estelle's hair as she trudged down Main Street. An hour has passed since Aubry had stormed from the library. Mrs. Ryskamp had offered to let her leave early, but there'd been no reason. In his current mood, he wouldn't welcome Estelle's chasing him down. How could the conversation turn hurtful so quickly?

She nibbled her lower lip as she gazed through the shop windows, barely taking in the displays. His quick temper was frightening. He'd never spoken to her in anger before the war, even when they disagreed. He was obviously suffering from more than physical wounds. Why couldn't countries get along? Why did they drag their young men into armed conflicts? She huffed out a breath. She knew exactly why: evil men like Hitler and Mussolini had to be stopped.

God must be crying as He looked down on the Earth He'd created. He'd given humanity a beautiful world in which to live, yet so many people didn't believe in Him. Thought they should own the world rather than act as the stewards they are.

She cringed as she shook her head. She was being judgmental. What had Jesus said? *Cast out the beam out of thine own eye, and then*

shall thou see clearly to cast out the mote out of thy brother's eye.
"Forgive me, Father. Help me help Aubry get better. Work a miracle in
him and take away the hurt and anger."

A woman passed and gave her an odd look.

Cheeks burning, Estelle shrugged. Hadn't the woman ever talked
to herself?

Estelle got to the end of the street and turned the corner. A boy
of about thirteen or fourteen swept the sidewalk in front of the market,
his red hair glistening in the midafternoon sunshine. A woman poked
through a display of tired-looking potatoes, a frown etching a deep V in
her forehead. Farther ahead, a couple strolled arm in arm, the woman
clinging to the man as if she never wanted to let him go. He wore a sling
around one arm and walked with a heavy limp. Which battle had caused
his injuries? Did he suffer in his mind, too? She blinked away tears that
welled in her eyes and threatened to tumble down her cheeks.

The door to the grocery popped open, and Mrs. Feeney hurried
outside. She said something to the young man who blushed and nodded
in response. The elderly woman had probably complimented him on the
good job he'd done. She had the gift of encouragement and sought
regular opportunities to uplift others.

Picking up her pace, Estelle waved to catch her friend's
attention. Mrs. Feeney must have sensed the motion because she looked
up, and her smile widened. She waited, pocketbook and canvas shopping
bag draped over her arm. Even at her advanced age, the woman insisted
on walking most places and carrying her own burdens.

"Mrs. Feeney, how nice to see you. Shopping so late?"

"You, too, dearie." Mrs. Feeney rolled her eyes. "Mr. Feeney has a hankering for sweet potato pie, although the idea of turning on the oven in this heat..." She giggled. "What am I saying? I never have been able to turn down one of his requests."

Estelle's eyes widened. The woman giggled like a schoolgirl, yet she and Mr. Feeney had to have been married nearly fifty years.

"Don't look so shocked, young lady. Just because I'm old, doesn't mean I have no emotions." She peered at Estelle. "Now, let's go find a nice bench to sit on, and you can tell me what's bothering you."

"How did you know?"

"I see the sadness lurking in your eyes. Is it Aubry?"

With a nod, Estelle reached for Mrs. Feeney's bag, "Let me carry that for you."

"Thank you, dear, it is a bit warm today."

They sauntered toward the town park, and Mrs. Feeney lowered herself on a worn wooden bench, then Estelle dropped beside her with a sigh. She'd spent very little time behind the circulation desk, instead walking the stacks to reshelve the books, and her feet throbbed.

With a few words, Estelle recounted the incident in the library. "I don't know what to do. He says he doesn't want to see me again. Can that possibly be true?"

"Could be, but I doubt it." Mrs. Feeney patted Estelle's arm. "We can't possibly understand what our men experienced over there. They barely understand it themselves, and then they come home and are expected to act like nothing happened. To just go back about their business. I would imagine the seriousness of war makes our lives on the home front seem petty."

"Then I should give him some time? Wait until he calls me?"

"Heavens, no." Mrs. Feeney brushed a piece of lint from her skirt. "You march up to his house and tell him you're there for your regular visit."

"He said he wanted to be alone. What if he throws me out?"

"Then you leave, but you go back the next day. And the next. Until he sees how much you care."

The clock tolled three o'clock, and Estelle jumped up from the bench, her heart racing. She bent to kiss the elderly woman's cheek. "Thank you, Mrs. Feeney. I usually visit Aubry at three o'clock, so I must run. You've given me hope, but I'd appreciate your prayers, especially this afternoon."

"I've never stopped praying for you, my girl. Ever since he went away." Eyes twinkling, she gave Estelle a nudge. "Be off with you, and give that boy my best, even if he doesn't want to hear it."

Pulse thrumming, Estelle rushed down the sidewalk. She'd be a few minutes late, but she'd be honest with Aubry and tell him she was reticent about coming, until her conversation with Mrs. Feeney. Would he be surprised? Was he still angry?

Give me the courage I need, Lord.

Peace, like a warm blanket, soothed her erratic thoughts, and she sighed. Why did she always forget to take problems and fears to her heavenly Father? Two turns later, and she'd arrived at the DeLuca house. She wiped damp palms on her skirt, then straightened her spine. Mrs. Feeney said to march, so she'd march.

The heels of her pumps clunked on the brick walkway as she approached the front door. She knocked on the door, then cringed as the noise reverberated inside the house. In her zealousness, she banged on the wood too loudly.

Footsteps sounded from inside, and the door swung open. Mrs. DeLuca grinned and stepped back. "He told me you weren't coming, but I knew better."

"How is he?"

"Feeling badly for having lost his temper."

"He told you?"

"Just enough."

Estelle held up the book she'd dug out of her purse. "We've got a new book to read."

"Good excuse." She wrapped Estelle in a quick embrace. "Get on in there, and I'll bring in some iced tea."

Heart in her throat, Estelle hurried to the living room.

Aubry's jaw dropped, and his eyebrow shot up almost to his hairline. "You came."

"I did, thanks to Mrs. Feeney." Estelle sat in the chair next to the sofa. "You know Mr. Feeney was at war, so they've been where we are." She swallowed. "Anyway, I won't pretend that I understand what you're dealing with, but you've accepted me. Why shouldn't I do the same for you? We liked each other before you left. A lot. I still like you. Can we start with that?"

He stared at her, myriad emotions flitting across his face.

She rubbed the book's cover as the silence lengthened. A nervous laugh burst out, and she coughed to cover the sound. "Listen, you don't need to answer right away, but I do have a favor to ask. I'm spearheading the book sale at the library, and I'd like your help. No one knows books like you do. I was going to pull together a committee, but I think you and I could easily handle it together." She winced and clamped her mouth closed. She was rambling, which was her habit when uneasy.

"Is this a charity job?"

"Yes, we'll be raising money for the war effort."

"I meant charity for me. To give me something to do."

"What?" She cocked her head. "No. If you'd rather not be involved, I'll ask someone else. I'm not sure what made me think of it, but I do need help." She knew exactly Who gave her the idea and had no doubt Mrs. Feeney's prayers were at work. God would get them through this, if only she could remember to let Him remain in charge.

CHAPTER TWELVE

Surrounded by dozens of boxes filled with books, Estelle twirled a lock of hair. The community had been more generous than she could have imagined, and she was running out of room. She'd already moved two of the children's bookcases, but she could only stack the cartons so high. Her gaze ran over the titles, and her fingers itched to pull out the volumes to study.

"You can't purchase them all." Aubry grinned, the corners of his eyes crinkling, his teeth flashing white against his dark beard. "Tempting as that is."

Her breath caught. Did he know how handsome he was? "But there are so many I haven't read yet."

"So many books, so little time, eh?"

"Exactly." She giggled, and her pulse tripped. Two days had passed since he'd agreed to help with the sale. They'd hung flyers around town yesterday morning, and by the time the library closed, the donations numbered in the hundreds. Mrs. Ryskamp had nearly skipped with joy when she saw the collection after she arrived. Estelle gave in to temptation and pulled out a book. "We need to begin organizing them.

We'll use alphabetical order for the fiction, but we should come up with broad categories for the nonfiction."

He clicked his heels, ignoring the pain in his thigh, and gave her an exaggerated salute. "Yes, ma'am." He pulled a folded sheet of paper from his pocket. "I've already given the matter some thought. Here are my suggestions."

She reached for the pages, and their fingers grazed, sending a jolt of electricity to her elbow. Had he felt anything? Since when did she react to his touch that way? She cleared her throat and shot him a saucy smile. "Well, haven't you been busy?"

Looking pleased, he shrugged. "Just trying to do my part."

"Now you know why I thought you were the best person for the job." She motioned to the two tables on his left. "We'll start by stacking them there, using the top of each table to start, then underneath.

Nodding, he lowered himself to the floor with a grunt, his long legs sticking out in front of him. He sifted through the nearest box, his strong hands gripping the books. The muscles in his forearms rippled with each movement.

Her mouth dried. What was wrong with her today? Her awareness of him had her heart pounding like a schoolgirl. She tore away her gaze and moved to the boxes at the far end of the room, then turned her back to him—the only way she'd be able to concentrate.

"Was it something I said?" His voice came from behind her.

Cheeks warm, she glanced over her shoulder and pinned a look of confusion on her face. "What do you mean?"

"I thought we'd work together, combining books as we went."

"Oh, of course. Good idea." She climbed to her feet and walked toward him. Would she be able to pay attention to her work? "Maybe you should be in charge." She kneeled next to him and tilted her head.

"Hardly, but thanks for the vote of confidence." He smirked and nudged her shoulder. "You'll do just fine. Oh, hey, I haven't read this one yet."

"Now, who's tempted?" She snickered.

Aubry chuckled, his face tinged with pink. He placed the volume on one of the growing stacks. "Do as I say, not as I do, eh?"

"Something like that." Estelle leaned forward to peer at the book's spine. *Brideshead Revisited?* I didn't know you were an Evelyn Waugh fan."

"He's a bit acidic, but I appreciate his satire. I read the book in college, then again last year. One of the boys had it, and we passed it around."

His expression turned distant, and Estelle stilled. He'd gone back to the war. Would he turn angry or sullen when he returned? Her stomach quivered.

Seconds later, he blinked and huffed out a sigh. "Sorry. You're going to fire me." The smile on his face appeared forced.

"Not going to happen." Eleanor handed him three slim volumes as tension slipped from her shoulders. He hadn't had an episode, as his mother referred to them. "These go with the Grace Livingstone Hill books."

"I'm not familiar with her."

"You're not exactly her target audience. She's a romance writer."

"I might read them."

"Uh-huh."

Aubry peered at the spines, then added the books to another teetering pile. He turned back to her. "Listen, thanks for not quizzing me about...things. It means a lot. You deserve to know what happened."

Tears gathered at the corners of her eyes, and she shook her head. "No. They're your private memories. If you never tell me, that's okay, but if you need to talk, I'm willing to listen."

He reached for her hand and laced his fingers with hers. "It was awful, and nothing prepared me...us, for it, even though they told us what to expect. There were guys who'd been at some pretty bloody battles, but they said Normandy trumped them all. I believe them."

The warmth of his palm spread up her arm, and she squeezed his hand, but refrained from commenting.

Raising his head, he met her gaze. "Why did I live, and why did some of them die? I'm no better than them and hopefully no worse. Why did God choose me?" He frowned. "Or was He even involved? It sure felt like He'd turned His back on us."

"I wish I had an answer for you. That's—"

"Well, isn't this sweet?"

Estelle yanked her hand from Aubry's and whipped around. "Francine."

"Gabbing isn't going to get the job done, and holding hands in public isn't appropriate." The librarian narrowed her eyes and gestured to the collection. "And you're hogging space in the children's area."

"Mrs. Ryskamp—"

"Mrs. Ryskamp doesn't know how much you goof off, but I plan to tell her. Sitting here and pretending to work. This is nothing but an excuse to be together. You've got her wrapped around your little finger." She crossed her arms and looked down her nose. "Why she put you in charge and not me is a mystery. Ridiculous. You don't have anywhere near my experience." Her gaze slid to Aubry. "And I can't imagine you're much help."

Estelle gasped at the veiled comment about Aubry's vision.

"Are you this charming to all the patrons?" Sarcasm colored his words

The woman's sneer faltered. "Just finish the job. The children will be here after school and will need the space."

"I'm aware of that."

Francine tapped her wristwatch. "Fine, but time is wasting." She spun on her heel and marched toward the circulation desk.

With tight lips, Estelle turned back to the box of books, studiously avoiding Aubry's incredulous expression. She pretended to read the titles as she struggled to regain control of her emotions. Anger, embarrassment, and hurt washed over her. Why was Francine so mean?

Aubry gritted his teeth and reached for Estelle's hand, but she pulled away. Her distraught was obvious. "Is she always this rude to you?" He barely spoke above a whisper. She was obviously upset but trying to mask her feelings, and he suppressed wanting to chase after the nasty woman and give her a piece of his mind. That move would only exacerbate the situation. He clenched his fists. Perhaps he was recovering after all. Two weeks ago, he would have followed through with his intentions.

With a deep sigh, Estelle wrapped her arms around her middle and studied the floor. "Ever since I started," she mumbled. "I don't know why. I've been nothing but respectful to her. Despite her claim, I don't goof off."

Using a gentle finger, he lifted her chin until she was forced to look at him. He might not be able to see her clearly, but pain emanated from her posture and downturned mouth. He snorted a harsh laugh as he stroked her jaw, the skin soft under his finger, then dropped his hand. "Take it from me; the problem is within her. Something is bugging her, and she's taking it out on you."

"But I didn't do anything to her."

"This is like when I lost my temper with you." His stomach hardened at the memories. "What you said triggered my response, but that doesn't mean it was your fault. I'm not explaining this well."

"I try to be polite, but it's hard. It seems as if she thinks I want to be more important than her. I don't. I'm not." She hunched deeper into herself. "I'm just a librarian who wants to help people find books to enjoy."

"And you do a fine job of that. Look how you've helped me." Another chuckle. "And I didn't want to be helped."

That got a smile out of her, and one corner of her mouth curved.

"Atta, girl." He puffed out his chest and grinned. He'd managed to improve her spirits. Mitch would be proud. Truth be told, he was proud of himself. "Now, I have a plan." He motioned to the floor. "I'll tell you about it while we finish sorting the books."

"Sounds intriguing." She knelt by one of the boxes. "I'm all ears."

He lowered himself beside her, his thigh only protesting with a slight twinge. He leaned close to Estelle's ear, and her floral scent filled his nose. His pulse tripped, and he swallowed. "I say we kill her with kindness."

She turned, her face a mere inch from his. "I already do that."

His gaze dropped to her lips, and he pulled back before he did something stupid. "I haven't been here, but from what you've said, I gather that you're polite in response to her nastiness. I'm suggesting you initiate conversations. Say good morning, if you don't already. Seek her opinion on things, even if you already know what you want to do. Chat about books you've enjoyed. Continue to offer to assist her with tasks. She'll be leery and question your motives."

Estelle's eyes widened. "But I do have a motive."

"Yes, a motive to get along and make her less of a pill." He handed her a book. "That's for the biography stack. Tell her you're just trying to get along. Tell her you're interested in what she has to say. Or just smile and shrug."

"I don't know—"

"The other part of the plan is to pray. Pray for her and pray about the situation." He gulped. Where had that come from? He was barely on speaking terms with God, yet he was handing out advice to seek the Lord's blessing and help. Talk about irony. Mitch would have a good laugh about this.

Her shoulders slumped. "You're right. I haven't taken the problem to God. I felt like He has bigger issues to deal with than the fact my coworker hates me."

"Trying to do it on your own." He squeezed her hand. "I wouldn't know anything about that." Where was all this confidence and wisdom coming from? *Is that You, Father?*

"Guilty as charged." She giggled like silver bells, and her cheeks pinked. "Will you pray for me, too?"

"Absolutely. We'll charge the gates of heaven. Together." *Here I come, Lord, ready or not. But I have a sneaking suspicion you're more than ready.*

Chapter Thirteen

Still three blocks away from the festivities, Estelle could hear the faint strains of music with the occasional thump of a drum. The buzz of conversation surrounded her as townspeople hurried past, each one carrying a metal object. Jostled from both sides, she threaded her way through the pedestrians to get close to the buildings.

She pulled a handkerchief from her pocket and blotted at the moisture on her face. Not even nine o'clock, and the temperatures must already be in the eighties, to say nothing of the typical Maryland humidity that thickened the air.

Across the street, Pastor Gibson and his wife stood in front of the market. He waved his arm. His wife looked up and beamed at her. Estelle waved in return, then checked the street before trotting to the other side.

"Can you believe this crowd?" Pastor Gibson rocked on his heels. "You'd think someone was giving something away instead of the other way around."

Estelle held up the crumpled watering can she'd found in the back of the garage. "At this stage of the war, I'm surprised we have anything to donate, but Dad drove over this last week. What did you bring?"

He opened his canvas bag to reveal two small cooking pots and a warped sheet pan. "We didn't have much around the house, either, but our troops have the Axis on the run, so perhaps our contributions won't be needed."

"Your mouth to God's ears," Mrs. Gibson said. "Selfishly, I'm glad that our son is too old to fight. I mourn for all the mothers who have lost their boys."

"My father said that Normandy broke the enemy's back, but that it might take another year to finish the conflict."

"Unfortunately, he's probably correct." Pastor Gibson tsked. "Speaking of that, how is your young man?"

"Better." She tucked a stray lock of hair behind her ear. "He's helping me with the upcoming book sale, which is forcing him out of the house. He was reticent at first, but seems more comfortable." She sighed. "People stare at him, Pastor Gibson. It's terrible. You'd think they were used to seeing our wounded men."

"You would, my dear, but we can't always count on others to do what is right." He patted her shoulder. "Does he have nightmares? Get angry?"

"Yes." Tears welled in her eyes. "I wish I could take them from him."

"You're a good girl, but he'll have to fight this demon on his own. Well, with God's help, of course. But you can always pray."

"I do. All the time, but it feels futile somehow."

"Understandable. You want to *do* something, some action, and you are. Prayer is one of the most powerful activities we can perform. Never forget that. God works through the prayers of His people."

"Yes, sir."

Pastor Gibson chuckled. "But you still want to do something. Nothing wrong with that, and you have, by asking him to lend a hand with the sale."

Estelle flushed. "True. I appreciate your encouragement."

"Are you meeting him here?"

"He wasn't sure if he was coming. Mrs. DeLuca is down with a summer cold, and he thought he should stay at home with her."

"Commendable."

The clock on the town hall struck the hour, the deep chimes resonating through the air and cutting off further conversation. Estelle pointed toward the end of the street, and the pastor gestured toward the grocery store. With a smile, she nodded and allowed herself to be swept up in the throng making its way toward the town center.

A few moments later, she arrived at the grassy park that sported a bandstand among several flower beds the town garden club maintained. She couldn't identify the plants but appreciated the colorful bobbing heads of the blossoms. A green thumb, she was not, although her grandfather had been a farmer, and his father before him.

Hundreds of people filled the expanse, and the clang of metal upon metal rang out as they tossed their items into the fenced area. In the white wood gazebo, a quartet of musicians played rollicking tunes. Several couples danced to the music while children chased each other among the adults. Except for the reason for the event, the party-like atmosphere made one think the war was over.

A small, balding man, the mayor, climbed the steps of the bandstand and raised his arms. No one seemed to notice, so he turned to the musicians, and the fiddler played a screeching note on his strings. Silence descended as the town's leader clasped his hands in front of himself and bestowed a benevolent smile at the upturned faces. "Welcome, and thank you for your generosity. We're sure to win the competition."

Cheers and applause punctuated the air.

He grinned and wiggled his eyebrows. "But we're not in it for the prize, right? We're doing this for the good of the war, right?"

The crowd laughed, and someone gave a piercing whistle.

"Seriously, folks, you've done well, and I'm proud of you. Laurel is the greatest little city in the nation. Dare I say it: the world. Now, I promise not to blather on, but I wanted to let you know you'll have another opportunity to do your bit, as they say. The library will be holding a book sale on Wednesday, the nineteenth. From what I hear, your generosity has overflowed, and there will be hundreds of books from which to choose."

He cleared his throat. "We are blessed that some of our servicemen have returned home, so there are heroes among us. Be sure to thank them. Because of their sacrifices, the war is nearly at its end." He motioned to the band. "Put on your dancing shoes, folks, because it's back to the grind on Monday." He waved and climbed down the steps and melted into the crowd.

Estelle wended her way through the throng toward the pile of donated scrap, the watering can clenched in one hand. The jumble of items towered above her as she tossed her contribution over the fence. The mayor was right about the residents' generosity. Several new-looking pieces were visible among the rusted and bent items.

Two women moved aside, revealing Aubry, who looked exceptionally handsome in gray slacks and a crisply ironed white shirt that contrasted with his tanned complexion. His dark hair glistened in the sun. More animated than she'd seen him since his return, he spoke with a buxom woman wearing a purple silk dress and matching hat. Estelle's lips twisted. Overdressed for the occasion, the woman obviously wanted to show off her wealth. Bad form when so many of the townspeople had pulled in their belts.

Who was she, and why would she be talking to Aubry?

Mouth dry, Estelle squared her shoulders and pinned on a smile, then pushed her way through the knots of people wandering the park.

Aubry glanced up, and their gaze met for a split second, then he said something to the woman in purple who nodded and walked away.

Estelle hesitated, then continued toward him.

"I'd hoped to see you here." He motioned to the tottering accumulation of metal and chuckled. "Who knew any of us still owned anything made of aluminum or steel?"

Estelle pursed her lips. He hadn't said anything about his conversation with the unknown woman. Dare she ask him? Would he tell her the truth? Was he trying to hide something, or was she jumping at shadows? Did she want to know?

Chapter Fourteen

Tucking her hands into the pockets of her skirt, Estelle studied Aubry's expression for clues. His jaw was set, and his smile seemed forced as he looked down at her. Because his pupil was still clouded, it was difficult to read his eye, but he seemed to be daring her to quiz him.

She pressed her lips against a sigh, then shrugged. Once again, Mrs. Feeney's words niggled at her: meet him where is he is and give him grace. What if she didn't want to? What if she wanted to have it out here and now? Would she always have to watch her words with him? How exhausting that would be.

Not normally the jealous type, Estelle was piqued by the fact he didn't say anything about the woman. Even casually. Would he care if he stumbled on her having a conversation with an unknown man? Or would he take it in stride?

Her chest tightened. He had a right to his life as she did with hers, but if they were going to be together, didn't they owe it to each other to be open? To share everything? Surely, her parents told each other everything? Would Aubry always cut off parts of himself from her? Would she have to accept that he held secrets?

"Estelle?" Aubry tilted his head. "You seem far away."

"What? Oh, I'm sorry." She shook her head. "It's nothing. What were you saying?"

"I said it's a wonder anyone owns anything made of metal these days."

"Yes, you're quite right. If Dad hadn't run over the watering can, we'd be hard pressed to find an item we can do without."

"Are you okay?"

"Why wouldn't I be?" She winced at the sharp edge in her voice. "I'm fine." Not really, but discussing the situation in public was not an option. "Were you able to rustle up anything to contribute?"

"We had a couple of rusted shovels. Not much, but better than nothing. I should probably rummage for more, but the idea of poking through the garage on such a beastly hot day held no allure."

Estelle fanned herself with one hand. "It is brutal, with no relief in sight. It's August, in Maryland, after all." So, they were relegated to discussing the weather. Fine. She'd play along. "The perfect day to be at the beach, but I guess that's out until after the war."

His eyebrow lifted, his expression still guarded. Apparently, he felt the awkwardness, too. "Yes, but by all accounts, it won't be long. Perhaps next summer will find us lounging on the sand."

"Perhaps." She lifted one shoulder. Time for a change in topic. "Did you hear the mayor announce the book sale? His plug for the event should bring in lots more potential customers. Good thing we're almost finished sorting the books."

One side of his mouth curved in a lopsided smile. "Unless his little advertisement brings in more donations."

"Ugh, I didn't think of that. What if we don't get all the volumes separated?"

Aubry tapped his chin with one finger, then brightened. "We could bundle the books and call it a grab bag. Tie them into bundles of four or five, using twine to make them look rustic."

"Brilliant. And if we don't get more, we can do that with the remaining unsorted books, allowing us to unload more of them."

"Now, you're talking."

He looked at her with pride, sending a thrill down her spine and washing away the last of her irritation at his silence about the mysterious woman. The band began a peppy rendition of Tommy Dorsey's "One O'Clock Jump," and Estelle's foot tapped to the rhythm. With his leg still healing, she couldn't expect a dance to this tune, but with any luck he'd be willing to try a turn around the field when a slow number came up. "Mrs. Griffee's daughter sent her maple syrup from Vermont, and she's offering snow cones. Wanna try one?"

"With sugar still rationed, that's a generous gift. I'd love one." He cleared his throat. "But before we do, you need to tell me what's wrong."

"Nothing."

"Maybe now, but when you came over, you seemed upset."

"You really have no idea?" Estelle put one hand on her hip and blew out a breath. "You can't think of one reason why?"

"No." His gaze slid past her. "I haven't seen you in two days. How could I have made you angry?"

Her stomach clenched. His unwillingness to meet her eyes said he was lying. He knew exactly why she was peeved, yet he was putting the onus on her to say it. He'd changed, and she wasn't sure she liked what he'd become. Cantankerous, secretive, and insensitive. He didn't seem to care something was bothering her, merely curious.

"Are you going to make me guess?" His eye narrowed, and he frowned. "That's not very sporting. I've never known you to sulk, Estelle. Why start now?"

"Excuse me?"

"You heard me. You didn't used to be so moody." He stuffed his hands into his pockets. "But you've got a bee in your bonnet about something, yet won't tell me so I can fix it. How's that fair? I'm not a mind reader."

"It shouldn't take a mind reader to figure out what's wrong." She poked his chest and hissed, "And you want to talk moody? Your mother and I have had to deal with your capricious disposition since you got home. I'm sorry you were wounded. I'm sorry you've lost vision in your eyes. I'm sorry for everything, but you act as if you're the only one who has been affected by this war. Men died. Lots of men, and plenty of families actually lost their loved ones. So, I think it's fair if I occasionally get a little out of sorts." Tears welled in her eyes as she glared at him, chest heaving.

Aubry's face reddened, and he glanced around.

"Worried about me being overheard? Well, if you didn't want an answer, Aubry, you shouldn't have asked the question."

"Estelle—"

She waved her hand in a dismissive gesture. "I'm suddenly very tired, Aubry. Enjoy your snow cone without me. I'm going home."

"But—"

"Goodbye, Aubry." Pain throbbed behind Estelle's left eye as she whirled, then marched toward the entrance to the park. Would he follow her? She shoved her way through the throng of people. Her mouth had run away with her face, and she should apologize for the terrible things she said to him. What sort of woman derides a man for struggling to deal with his injuries? Injuries that impacted his quality of life. He must think her a shrew. Think, nothing. She was a shrew. He deserved better than her. Some woman who could coddle him and keep a civil tongue in her head. She'd called his mood capricious, and she'd acted the same way, her emotions ricocheting like one of those Australian boomerangs she'd read about.

Her chin trembled. She'd ruined everything, and there was no turning back.

CHAPTER FIFTEEN

Rubbing his forehead, Aubry huffed out a loud breath and watched Estelle's form until she melted into the crowd. Her words echoed in his mind, and he frowned. Of course, he knew men died. He'd been there. He'd lost too many friends to count. He blinked and scuffed the grass with one foot. He didn't think he was the only one who suffered. How could she say that?

Snippets of his comments since being home pushed their way into his head, and a chill swept over him despite the day's high temperatures. Instances of being less than cordial to his mother, verbally shoving away her attempts at cheering him. Times he'd been snippy with Estelle. Perhaps he had been crabby, but they didn't understand. His whole life had tumbled down around him on that beach, the shrapnel tearing away promises of a bright future.

With a frown, he pivoted. Where to go? Not home. He'd have to explain to his mother why he was there early. He tossed a glance over his shoulder. Should he seek out Estelle and apologize? He still didn't know what he'd done to set her off, but Mitch would tell him it didn't matter. That, as a man, he had a responsibility to smooth things over.

Mitch. He'd lost a leg, yet approached life with grace and humor. He had a job that allowed him to provide for himself and his family. Were there really possible positions for a man with clouded vision? No. There were too many applicants who could see. They'd come first.

He turned around and collided with an elderly woman with snow-white hair. Her blue eyes sparkled in her lined face. He gripped her arms to keep her from falling. "Pardon me." Recognition dawned. "Mrs. Feeney, I'm sorry for bumping into you. I was, um, distracted." He released her and crossed his arms.

She kissed his cheek, then squeezed his shoulder. "Welcome home, Aubry. It's wonderful to see you. Your mother and I prayed every night for your safe return, and here you are. God is good, isn't He?"

"Ah, sure." He rocked on his heels. "Are you alone? Where's Mr. Feeney?" He gulped. He shouldn't have asked. The old man may have died in the last two years.

"Puttering in the garden. He hates crowds." She beamed, then slipped her hand into the bend of his right arm and tugged. "Walk with me."

"Well, I—"

"We won't be long. I thought a little chat was in order."

"All right." He motioned forward. "Lead on. You seem to have a destination in mind."

The elderly woman grinned. "Just a spin around the edge of the festivities. I don't mind the vast number of people, but the noise makes conversation a challenge. Don't you agree?"

"Yes." He'd agree to anything she said at this point. She obviously had an agenda, and the sooner that surfaced, the better.

They walked in silence for a couple of minutes, and Aubry tried to study the woman out of the corner of his eye. With a start, he realized his vision wasn't as blurred. His heart pounded. Would he regain his sight entirely?

"Thank you for giving in to the demands of an old lady you barely know." She squeezed his arm. "You're a good boy."

He snorted a laugh. "At thirty-one, I'm hardly a boy, Mrs. Feeney."

"From where I stand, you are." She winked. "But enough about that. It's nice to see you smile. I'm sure the adjustment of being home is difficult. You couldn't wait to get here, but everything is a jumble of being different, yet the same."

"How could you—"

"Mr. Feeney was in the last two wars. He was older for both, like you. First the conflict in Cuba against the Spanish, then the one they're calling the Great War." She scoffed. "Nothing great about it. He carried a gun for the first one and drove an ambulance for the second. The result was the same. He was a changed man."

Aubry shuddered. He'd heard about the trench warfare during the last war. Most of the officers he served under had been there. They spoke of the gasses that killed and maimed, ruining a man's lungs for life. No-man's-land. Bayonets and hand-to-hand fighting. "I didn't know."

"He was well aware of the futility and horrific carnage of war from his time in Cuba, but felt called to serve in the last one. Called by God is what he said. I had a hard time believing that. He had two girls who needed their daddy. I said some terrible things before he left, then spent the rest of the war writing letters filled with apologies."

"Worry makes us say things we don't mean."

"A wise man." She smoothed her skirts. "God was good and saw fit to send him home unscathed. Physically, anyway. He had nightmares for years. Still does on occasion."

"How long?"

"How long did it take him to recover?" She sighed. "Too long. When he finally talked about it with our pastor, he began to get better. You see, back then, men were expected to have the proverbial stiff upper lip. If someone was overcome by what he saw, it was called lack of moral fiber. Now the doctors call it battle fatigue. The mind can only take so much. We know that now. You need to find someone to talk to. It will be painful, but it will help."

Aubry's chest was tight, and he shrugged.

"You feel guilty about surviving, and you're angry your friends had to die. There's nothing wrong with those feelings, but you must work through them. The gracious and kind young man I knew is still in there, but you'll have to break down the walls to let him out." She stroked his arm and shot him a saucy smile. "Now, while I'm being a busybody, tell me about Estelle. How is she dealing with all of this?"

"She's struggling. We, uh, just had an argument."

"Surprised you, didn't she? She's had to grow up, seeing the man she loves go off to war, knowing he might not come back. Our girl has changed...matured, but she's also the same inside. Think about what drew you to her in the first place. You'll find it if you look hard enough, but you have to make a choice as to whether to accept this new version of her." Mrs. Feeney pulled his head down and kissed his cheek again. "Now, I'll leave you to think about what I said. And I'll be praying for the both of you."

He gaped at her as she sauntered off. Had she sought him out or just happened to see him? She was mother's best friend. No wonder she knew about his—what did she call them—difficulties. Instead of making him angry, her words had acted as a balm to his ravaged soul. She spoke to him without judgment, yet shined the light on his behaviors. He owed his mother an apology. Estelle, too. Would she forgive him?

Chapter Sixteen

Perspiration trickled down Estelle's spine as she hunched over the table tying twine around a trio of Grace Livingston Hill books. The windows were open, but no breeze fluttered the curtains, and the temperature inside the library climbed as the morning progressed. Francine was in the back accessioning books, and Mrs. Ryskamp worked the desk. An elderly man sat in one of the rockers reading the newspaper while two women strolled the aisles.

Glancing periodically at the door, Estelle frowned. Would Aubry show up to help as promised? After her scathing remarks, he had no reason to want to be with her, even if it meant the book sale would be more difficult. A damp lock of hair dangled on the side of her face, and she tucked it behind her ear. She should probably go to the break room and check her appearance. Heat and humidity always wreaked havoc with her curls, giving them more of a mind of their own than usual.

She snipped another piece of twine, then wrapped the cord around another stack. The tedium of the task allowed too much room in her head to think. *Father, forgive my anger at Aubry. Help him to forgive me. I know he can't forget my sharp words, but help him overlook them.*

If he didn't appear by the end of the day, she'd go to his house. She should have done so two days ago, but her embarrassment and the thought he might not be willing to see her kept her cowering at home.

Yesterday's headache had been the perfect excuse to skip church, although being alone in her stuffy bedroom avoiding him hadn't done anything to relieve the throbbing. Instead, memories and self-recrimination assailed her. She'd finally fallen into a fitful sleep interrupted by confusing dreams.

The front door opened, brightening the room for a brief moment. Aubry's uneven gait sounded, and her stomach hollowed. He'd come. Even after all she'd said. Her chin trembled. He cared enough about the project to set aside his feelings.

"Good morning, miss. Can I lend you a hand?" His voice was warm and held a hint of humor.

Her pulse raced, and she clenched her hands to cease their trembling. Turning, she blinked away the tears. "Aubry, you came. In spite of everything, you came."

A tentative smile hovered on his face. "I should have gone to your house after...you know...but I wasn't sure you'd see me."

"I am so—"

He held up a hand. "Please, don't say you're sorry. It's me who should apologize. Will you forgive my beastly behavior?"

"Forgive you? But I'm the one who was mean."

"Only after reaching your wit's end. Mitch said it would be hard to go home, to adjust to...everything, but I was arrogant and thought I could handle it. Boy, was I wrong." He raked his fingers through his lengthening hair. "I visited Mr. and Mrs. Feeney. She collared me at the scrap drive. Said a lot of things that got me thinking. Did you know Mr. Feeney was in two wars? One was plenty for me. Anyway, I went to their house, and we talked for a long time. And prayed. I can't promise I won't have bad moments, but I've realized God didn't do this to me as some sort of cosmic joke or punishment. That He chose to let me live, and I've got to make the most of the life He's given me." He fell silent, and his smile faltered.

Estelle resisted the urge to throw her arms around him, instead grabbing his hands and grinning liked she'd won a year's supply of sugar. "Oh, Aubry. That's wonderful. I'm so pleased for you. God is good, isn't He?"

"He is, indeed." Aubry's smile bloomed, and he cocked his head. "So does that mean you forgive me?"

A giggle burst from her lips. "Of course, but you must forgive me, too. I may have been angry, but that didn't give me the right to say hateful things."

"You're forgiven." He squeezed her fingers. "Now, did you leave any of the fun for me?"

"Absolutely. I'm almost done with sorting, so you can start taking boxes back to the storeroom."

He put two fingers to his forehead in an exaggerated salute, then clicked his heels. "Yes, ma'am."

She rolled her eyes and swatted his shoulder. *Thank You, Lord!*

"Are you about done with this mess?"

Estelle whirled.

Francine stood, hands on her hips and a deep scowl on her face. "You promised to clear out last week, yet here we are."

"As a matter of fact, we just discussed that very thing, Miss O'Malley. We apologize for not meeting your deadline. Thoughtless of us, really. After all, you've got a library to run. I shouldn't be more than twenty to thirty minutes. The townspeople have been quite generous, you see, and we have more cartons than anticipated."

The woman lifted her chin and preened. "I don't exactly run the library, but my job is important. Exhausting sometimes."

Closing her eyes to keep from rolling them, Estelle swallowed a retort. Better to let Aubry handle her difficult coworker.

"Of course it is. All those responsibilities. *I* couldn't do it." Aubry picked up one of the boxes. "How about if you show me where to stow these?"

"Certainly, follow me." Cheeks pink, Francine glanced at Estelle. "This was a huge undertaking. You've done a good job."

Mouth agape, Estelle watched them make their way across the library, then behind the circulation desk before disappearing into the staff area. Francine had been less prickly since Estelle had taken Aubry's suggestion and tried to be extra cordial and seeking her coworker's advice, but this was the first time the woman had actually initiated a compliment. And was that a blush on her face? Would wonders never cease?

Estelle continued to bundle the last of the loose books as Aubry took the filled boxes into the storeroom. He'd nearly finished when Francine returned with a cup of water. "You must be quite parched, Mr. DeLuca."

"How kind of you, Miss O'Malley." He reached for the glass, then downed the liquid in one long gulp. "Thank you for thinking of me, what with all you have to do."

"No, thank *you*." She fluttered her eyelashes. "It's nice to have a man around to do the heavy lifting." She turned to Estelle. "We should ask Mrs. Ryskamp to hire him."

For the second time, Estelle found herself slack-jawed.

Aubry handed Francine the glass. "I'm fine volunteering, Miss O'Malley, but I appreciate the offer. Anytime you need something carried, give me a call."

Francine giggled and shook her head as she made her way back to the circulation desk.

"Who is that woman?" Estelle widened her eyes. "And may we keep her?"

Chuckling, Aubry hefted another carton into his arms. "See what a little kindness does?"

"Any more *kind*, and she may develop a crush on you, if she hasn't already."

"Nope. You're the only gal for me." Still laughing, Aubry strolled away.

Estelle swallowed. Was he serious or merely caught up in the hilarity of the moment? She wasn't sure she wanted the answer.

CHAPTER SEVENTEEN

Humming as he carried the heavy carton to the closet, Aubry nodded to Mrs. Ryskamp as he walked past her office. Had the woman heard the exchange with Miss O'Malley? The library director had been at the circulation desk during the conversation. Her expression was pleasant and noncommittal, but he had a feeling she would make an excellent poker player if given the chance. Working with the public, she'd probably learned to hide her thoughts. Whereas, Estelle wore her emotions close to the surface.

She tried to school her features. He'd seen her try but without much luck. She'd looked adorable as she stared at Miss O'Malley. Shock, amazement, then amusement as the librarian had batted her eyelashes in an awkward attempt at flirtation. He might have snickered had he not recognized the emptiness within the woman. Did she have any friends? Did her prickliness put people off? It was probably a shield very much like his own. He'd need to discuss that with Estelle but without sounding condescending. He'd learned his lesson about how he often came across.

A sigh slipped out as he put the box on the shelf. Helping Estelle smooth her relationship with the woman felt good as did being her able-bodied assistant with the book sale. Working with her gave him a reason to get up and out of the house, but the tasks were hardly challenging, at least mentally. Although mostly healed, the scar on his thigh throbbed by nightfall and was worse on the days he came to the library, but he'd never let on to her, or she'd insist he rest. His eye burned after hours of peering at book titles, but he wouldn't tell her that, either.

How would he ever hold a full-time job if volunteering for a few hours here and there wore him out? He'd never be able to provide for a family if he couldn't build up his stamina. And his vision. In the last few days, he'd seen...if he could use that word...an infinitesimal improvement but hardly anything to celebrate. His sight was still as if he were looking at life through waxed paper. No, more like a window that teemed with water during a storm.

When would he hear back from the woman he'd run into at the scrap drive? She claimed to be a sister to one of his buddy's from college, but he hadn't recognized her. She said she met a local from Laurel at Western Maryland and married the man. She worked at Meade while he was away. He'd enlisted in the navy before they could draft him. Said he wanted to choose how he did his part. The woman worked for some sort of secret government agency but wouldn't tell him which one. The organization was looking for seasoned veterans to give them a hand. He told her he'd already done enough, but she said she'd be back. Was that good or bad?

How long would he have to wait to hear from her, and did they really want a veteran, no matter how banged up?

He rubbed his thigh and grimaced. Mitch would tell him he was borrowing trouble by worrying about the future. "Sorry, Lord. I know You've got a plan, but I'd sure like to know what it is. Can You give me some sort of sign that You haven't forgotten me?"

"Mr. DeLuca? Are you okay in there?"

Aubry's face heated. Had the director heard his prayer? Did she think he was talking to himself? Did she think him crazy? "Coming, Mrs. Ryskamp." He strode from the storeroom, then stopped in her doorway. "Did you need something or wonder if I got lost?"

"A little of both." She smiled. "I wanted to thank you for giving us a hand. We could do this on our own, but you're making it so much easier. I'm sure you'd rather be working, so I appreciate your time."

"I'm happy to provide assistance." He shrugged. "I haven't been able to find a job yet, so it's no problem."

"Don't be discouraged. You haven't been home all that long. Something will turn up." She folded her hands. "Besides, you've got the rest of your life to be at work. Enjoy the leisure while you can."

"Yes, ma'am."

"Your degree is in finance, right? My cousin's husband works at one of the banks in town. I'll see if they're hiring. They must be able to use a bright young man like you."

He tilted his head, and his eyebrows rose. "How do you know my field of study?"

"Small town and too many hours in a library where people talk about *everything*. Even topics that are none of their business."

"Ah, of course." He dipped his head. "Don't put yourself out on my account. I'll find something soon enough." With a wave, he continued down the corridor. But how soon?

Even if he did obtain a job, men who hadn't been damaged in the war would come home. Surely, they would get first dibs. For work and women. His gut tightened. Estelle deserved someone whole. Someone she wouldn't have to chauffeur around because he couldn't see to drive. Someone she wouldn't have to slow down for because he couldn't walk great distances. Someone who could tell her of her beauty, and she'd know he meant it because the man could actually see her loveliness. Bah! He was wallowing in self-pity again, and he'd promised himself, and God, he'd stop.

Pinning a smile on his face, he straightened his spine as he approached Estelle.

She looked up. "Did you get lost?"

His pulse quickened. "Mrs. Ryskamp asked me the same thing right before she offered to be on the lookout for job possibilities."

Squealing, she clapped a hand over her mouth for a brief second, then said, "Oh, Aubry, that's wonderful. She's a peach, isn't she?"

He chuckled. "This is a library, you know."

"I'm not going to honor that with an answer." She nudged his shoulder, then motioned to the final box. "If you'll grab that, I can carry the bag."

"Fair enough." He stooped and picked up the box with an exaggerated groan. "I think I've caught my limit."

"You're not lifting correctly. Haven't you seen the Jenny on the Job posters?"

"I guess not. Who's she? Does she work here?"

"No, silly. The posters came out last year. The Public Health Service must have though we ladies needed some education and encouragement. But apparently you do, too."

"Cute." He wrinkled his nose, then jerked his head toward the desk. "Lead on."

Her scent wafted toward him as he followed her. She walked to the storeroom, then stepped aside so he could enter first. He set the box on one of the stacks and turned to her as her foot snagged the threshold. She pitched forward, and he caught her in his arms. Her face was close, so close she was barely blurred. He lowered his head, gently brushing his lips against hers.

CHAPTER EIGHTEEN

Estelle's arms slipped around Aubry's waist as his heart pounded against her chest, sending her pulse into a rapid dance. His lips were warm and gentle, yet firm as his aroma of bay rum and soap enveloped her. Her eyes fluttered closed as she lost herself in the moment. His beard tickled her skin, and her toes curled. His kisses had never felt like this before he left.

A noise sounded in the hallway, and they sprang apart. Her face burned, and she gulped. Her lips tingled as she turned and pretended to busy herself among the boxes. Her mouth dry, she swallowed. Did he care for her more than she'd thought, or had he been caught up in the moment?

"I've got an errand to run, Estelle." Mrs. Ryskamp appeared in the doorway. "I won't be long, but you'll need to give Francine a hand at the desk when the schoolchildren arrive."

"Yes, ma'am." Estelle motioned to the boxes. "We've finished sorting and are as ready as we'll ever be for the sale."

"Excellent." One eyebrow raised, the director's gaze slid to Aubry, then back to Estelle. "We can discuss logistics when I return."

Estelle nodded. Did she look different? Did Mrs. Ryskamp know she'd nearly caught them in an embrace. No, more than an embrace. Would she reprimand Estelle later?

"Do you need any help, Mrs. Ryskamp?" Aubry grinned. "According to Miss O'Malley, I'm handy to have around for lifting."

The woman chuckled. "Good to know, but I'm fine." She turned, and her footsteps faded.

Ducking her head, Estelle fled the closet. She hurried down the corridor, then entered the main room. Was her face as red as it felt? Would Francine surmise something had happened? She cleared her throat. "Aubry and I have stowed the books, so the kid's area is cleared."

"Is he still here? We need to put out the chairs and rug for story time."

Aubry emerged from the hallway. "I can do that. Just point me to where I'd find the items." He glanced at Francine, then pierced Estelle with a look. A look filled with mixed emotions, all of which she couldn't read.

Francine hopped off the stool. "Follow me. I'll show you."

Estelle smoothed her skirts and returned his gaze, her stomach quivering. "Thanks, Francine. I'll man the desk."

They sauntered away, and Estelle's breath rushed out. Her knees were weak as she climbed onto the stool Francine had vacated. She

130

touched her mouth with a quivering hand. She'd shared a handful of kisses with Aubry before he'd been drafted, but none of them had sent shivers down her spine or provoked feelings of desire. She'd responded and leaned into him, pulling him toward her. Electricity had shot to her fingertips and toes, and she'd wanted to stay cocooned in his embrace forever. To tell him of her love.

Moisture sprang out on her palms, and she froze as the word pushed its way forward in her mind. Her lips curved. She did love him. Somewhere in the midst of working on the mundane task of preparing for the sale, the evenings spent in his living room reading aloud, and a few Sundays sitting side by side in the pew, she'd fallen in love with him. Fully and hopelessly in love with him.

How could it have happened? It wasn't as if he'd wooed her with compliments and sweet words. They'd discussed books and sorted books. They'd sat in silence, drinking in the pastor's sermon. And they'd argued. Heatedly. Is that what love and marriage were made of?

She rubbed her forehead. Her parents rarely disagreed. Or had they hidden their contention?

Despite nearing thirty, she had little experience with men. She'd focused on her studies in college, and most of the guys had fallen into two categories: childish or shallow, wanting relationships that consisted of carousing and cuddling.

Shuddering, she reached into the book drop and pulled out the remaining four volumes that had been returned. She rifled through the file of checkout cards, then slipped them into the pockets of each book.

Aubry's demeanor had drawn her like a hummingbird to sugar water. His keen intelligence coupled with a clever sense of humor had resonated with her. His handsome face covered with a closely cropped beard, dark hair, and gray eyes were an added bonus.

He'd initiated the kiss, but was he shocked at her unspoken request to prolong the kiss? He seemed to enjoy it. She touched her lips again. She certainly did. Perhaps a bit too much.

Aubry followed Miss O'Malley to the corner of the children's area, listening to her chatter with half a mind. The woman's behavior had changed from dour to effervescent, which was nice to see, but now she talked nonstop. She opened the door and gestured to a rolled-up rug in the back and three stacks of small, child-sized chairs.

"Lay out the rug, then arrange the chairs in a circle, leaving room for my stool." She smiled. "And a chair for yourself, if you'd like to join us."

"Uh, no, thank you. I need to leave shortly."

Hands on her hips, the librarian tilted her head and snickered. "Kids not your cup of tea? You're going to have to get used to them sooner or later. You and Estelle are headed for the altar, so little ones are in your future. Perhaps the not-so-distant future."

He gaped at her, then cleared his throat. "That's not it. I have things to do."

"Whatever you say." She winked and whirled, her dress swishing as she walked away, her soft laughter continuing.

Headed for the altar? Children? His mind tumbled as he went into the closet and wrestled the rug from the corner. He dragged it to the center of the space, then dropped it with a thud. He squatted and unfurled the heavy carpet. Panting, he winced as his thigh clenched with the effort. Returning to the closet, he grabbed a pair of chairs and carried them to the rug. Back and forth he trudged, trying to ignore the discomfort in his leg. If he didn't get home soon and give it a rest, he wouldn't be able to walk tomorrow.

Did Estelle think they were serious enough to marry? Surely not. They'd enjoyed each other's company, but they'd also fought. Vehemently. He'd said things. Hurtful things. And so had she. But arguing didn't mean they didn't care. His parents had bickered, but underneath the squabbling had been love and mutual respect. Sometimes, it seemed his father would verbally poke his mother just to get her riled, so he could then sweep her into his arms and shower her with kisses, embarrassing Aubry and causing his mother to giggle like a schoolgirl.

He smiled at the memories, but his heart tugged. Papa had been gone seventeen years already. Taken too soon. Bah! He was avoiding the issue. He'd kissed Estelle and liked it. Very much.

He hadn't meant to, but she'd been right there. So close and looking so beautiful. Her lips plump and pink, her eyes wide. Her skin was pale, even more so in contrast to her cinnamon-brown hair. His pulse had thundered with the feel of her in his arms, then he'd caught a whiff of her rosewater, and before he could chicken out, he'd kissed her.

They'd exchanged a few chaste kisses before he left, but they had been nothing like this. Nothing at all. She'd tasted of sunshine and peppermint, and her lips had been as delicate as he'd imagined. After a split second of stiffness, they'd warmed and welcomed him.

Nonetheless, he couldn't guarantee that she didn't think him a cad. An opportunist. What sort of man steals a kiss in a closet, of all places? Not exactly the romantic moment every woman dreamed of. He hadn't planned to kiss her, but perhaps that was the problem. He'd been avoiding the truth. She'd begun to mean more to him than he wanted to admit.

His mother would be thrilled. She loved Estelle, lighting up whenever she came to visit. They chatted like best friends. Why should he be surprised? They'd had more than two years together without him. To worry and wait.

What to do?

He completed creating the circle with the last two chairs and stepped back to survey the arrangement, then straightened a couple of seats that were out of alignment. He rolled his eyes at his attempt at perfection. The little devils would have the chairs all hurly-burly moments after they arrived.

Huffing out a sigh, Aubry finger-combed his hair, then tugged at his collar. He'd stalled long enough. He massaged his thigh as he walked, his limp more pronounced than usual. Yep, he was going to pay for his activities tomorrow, but he wouldn't change a thing.

"All set, Miss O'Malley." He spoke to the librarian, but his gaze strayed to Estelle who stood with her back to them, arranging books on a wheeled cart.

"Thank you. A lifesaver, as always."

"Anytime." Aubry nodded, still staring at Estelle. A ray of sunlight came through the window and fell across her, creating a halo and making her hair glisten and sparkle. What would it be like to pull the pins from her victory rolls and bury his face into the dark tresses?

A dangerous line of thought. He pulled away his gaze and looked at Miss O'Malley, who smirked at him. His face warmed. He'd been caught staring like some addlepated boy in short pants. Now what?

CHAPTER NINETEEN

Three hours later, Aubry returned to the library. A blur of color greeted him from the gardens where someone had planted dozens of pink and purple flowers amid the shrubs. A hot breeze made the blossoms dance. He pulled out his handkerchief and blotted at the perspiration on his face. As he returned the hanky to his pocket, he glanced up at the cloudless sky. The sun had dipped toward the trees, but its suffocating heat remained. Oh, for the cooler days of October.

He stood on the sidewalk and studied the building. A woman came through the door and nodded as she passed. Had he imagined it, or had she given him a wide berth? He frowned. He had to stop worrying about what others thought of his appearance. Yeah, that was going to happen.

With a sigh, he straightened his spine. Would Estelle be glad to see him? He hadn't said he'd come back. He'd stayed for a few minutes after the kiss, but lack of privacy prevented any discussion about it, and she'd obviously been unsettled. Even with his poor vision, her skittishness had been apparent, so he'd made an excuse and left.

Myriad emotions had dogged him since then, until his mother told him he needed to handle whatever was bothering him. So much for thinking he'd hidden his feelings. Fortunately, she hadn't peppered him with questions, but he'd had enough for both of them.

"Hey, mister, are you a pirate?"

"Jimmy!"

Aubry started and looked into the embarrassed face of a young woman, then down at a small boy of perhaps five or six years old. No, maybe more. The child was missing one of his front teeth.

"I'm just wondering, Ma." The boy looked curious and not the least bit frightened. "Well, are you?"

Chuckling, Aubry ruffled the boy's hair. "No, I'm not, but I guess I look like one, huh?"

"Yeah, I read about them in a book, and pirates wear patches just like you." Jimmy crossed his arms. "Is your eye under there or did you lose it?"

"Jimmy! I'm so sorry, sir. He doesn't mean anything by his questions."

"No need to apologize." Aubry smiled and realized he meant what he said. He wasn't offended or upset. He'd have to think about that later. "I still have my eye, but it's badly damaged, not pretty to look at, so I cover it with the patch."

"How'd you get hurt?"

Aubry squatted so he could be close to the boy. "I was in the war."

"Oh, you are a soldier. My daddy's in the war. Maybe he'll get to come home with a patch."

"Maybe." Aubry pursed his lips. Hardly something Jimmy's father would desire, but the boy was too young to understand.

"I think you look swell." Jimmy tossed a glance at his mother. "I wanna make me one when we get home."

"Which is where we should be going." She gripped Jimmy's shoulder. "Say goodbye to Mr...?"

"DeLuca. Aubry DeLuca." He rose. "I hope to see you again, Jimmy."

The boy grinned and waved. "Goodbye, Mr. DeLuca. I like the library. If you come here, you'll see me."

"Thank you for...well, just thank you." The boy's mother smiled.

"You're welcome. And I'll pray for your husband's safe return. Without..." Aubry motioned toward his patch. "You know...this."

"I'd take him any way he came." She led Jimmy down the street, the boy's chatter fading as the distance between them and Aubry grew.

He shook his head. That woman had her hands full with that little man. She'd been mortified, but the boy's honest curiosity hadn't set off Aubry's anger that usually surged when someone stared or recoiled. He grinned. Jimmy said he looked "swell," and his words had acted as a salve. Mitch would get a kick out of the fact that a child had made a chink in the wall.

The door to the library opened, and Estelle and Francine walked outside. Estelle stopped. "Aubry? What are you doing here?"

"I, uh, thought I'd escort you home. It's a beautiful day for a walk."

Francine laughed. "No, it's not. It's beastly out."

Estelle giggled. "She's right."

"Guess I'm lucky it's not too far, eh?" He shrugged. "But I'd like to take you, if you'll allow me."

Francine leaned close to Estelle. "I say you take him up on the offer. Someone else will snap him up if you don't."

Cheeks pink, Estelle nodded, then waved at Francine. "See you tomorrow."

"Have fun, you two." Francine waggled her eyebrows, then turned in the opposite direction.

"I can hardly believe the change in her." Estelle tucked her pocketbook under her arm as they started walking. "It's like there was never any contention."

"I'm glad for you. Must make the days at worker easier."

"Incredibly so."

They strolled along the tree-lined sidewalk in silence for several minutes. Every now and then, the breeze would waft Estelle's floral
140

scent toward him. She'd gone with lilac today. Sweet, light, just like her. They were almost to her house.

"Listen, about earlier...you know...the closet...the kiss." He jammed his hands into his pockets. "I'm sorry for that. Not that it wasn't wonderful, but I was out of line."

She seemed to study the ground as they sauntered along the sidewalk. "You don't have to apologize. You're probably lonely."

"That sounds like I go around kissing anyone."

"What? No, that's not what I meant." The rose in her cheeks deepened. "I'm—"

"Trying to give me an excuse? A reason?" He put his hand on her arm to stop their progress. "You're special. I kissed you because I want to kiss *you*, not anyone else."

"That's nice of you to say, but I know you're just relieved to be home and happy to see me. I've enjoyed our time together renewing our friendship." She flashed a look at her house, then back at him. "I won't hold you to any sort of promise. You don't have to worry that I think there's more to this than there is." She kissed his cheek. "Thanks for walking me home."

Estelle hurried up the walkway, then into the house without a backward glance. The door closed with a soft thud.

Eyes wide, he gaped at the house. What had just happened?

Chapter Twenty

Estelle eased the door closed, then winced when the hinge squeaked. She'd hoped to sneak upstairs to her room for a few minutes of solitude. She'd never been good at hiding her emotions, so one look, and her mother would know something was amiss.

"Is that you, dear?" Her mother's voice floated down the hall from the kitchen.

"Yes, ma'am." So much for escaping her mother's scrutiny.

"Dinner is nearly ready." Estelle's mother poked her head around the corner. "I haven't had a chance to set the table."

Hanging her pocketbook on the newel post, Estelle forced a smile and nodded, then headed into the kitchen, sweltering with heat. A fan in the corner barely moved the stifling air. "I can do that. Where's Dad?"

"In the garage, something to do with the car." Her mother raised one eyebrow. "Is everything all right? You look...harried."

"Long day, that's all." Estelle collected plates and silverware, then went to the dining room and laid out the items on the table. She went back into the kitchen to grab napkins. She inhaled deeply. "Smells delicious."

"Vegetable soup, and I made bread. That's why it's so hot in here. Bad decision on my part."

"It will be worth it."

Footsteps sounded, and a moment later, Estelle's father clomped into the kitchen, wiping grease-stained hands on a rag. "Well, that took longer than anticipated. Hello, sweetie. Good day?"

"Yes." She turned on the spigot, then stepped back so he could wash his hands. "What's wrong with the car?"

"Running rough. I was hoping it was a quick fix, but I'm going to have to take the vehicle to the garage. The timing's off." He yanked the towel from the handle on the oven door, then pecked her mother on the cheek. She swatted at him but missed as he spiraled out of the way. He winked at Estelle. "Can't blame a guy for wanting a little love."

Her mother giggled. "No, but *your* timing's off."

Her dad guffawed and tossed the towel on the counter. "That's why I married your mom, Estelle. She always keeps me laughing."

"No one else would have you."

He chuckled and pressed both hands to his chest in mock despair. "Ouch!"

Estelle rolled her eyes. Her parents always teased each other, but tonight seemed exceptionally corny. Were they putting on a show on her behalf?

The timer pinged, and her mother shooed them out of the way. She opened the oven and pulled out a sheet pan filled with rolls, then set it on a metal cooling rack. "We'll serve ourselves from the stove tonight, so grab a bowl." She dumped the steaming bread into a waiting basket, then dunked a ladle into the soup pot.

"After you, ladies." Dad bowed low.

Moments later, the three of them carried their food into the dining room and seated themselves. Dad said grace, and they began to eat.

A comfortable silence blanketed the room, and about the time Estelle thought she'd get away without discussing her love life, her mother piped up. "How is Aubry doing these days? We should have him over for dinner. And soon."

"Good." Estelle wiped her mouth on the napkin. "He's been a huge help preparing for tomorrow's book sale. I don't think I'd be ready if it wasn't for him."

"He's a nice boy. I'm glad he made it home."

"Mother, he's thirty-one. Hardly a boy."

"He is, from my vantage point. Anyway, I'm pleased you're seeing him again. War can ruin a relationship."

"We're just friends." Estelle's face warmed.

"Not based on that look." Her dad grinned, then sobered. "But honestly, the best marriages are built on friendship. That's the way your mother and I started, and it's been the foundation for us. Not only do we love each other, we *like* each other. We want to spend time together. It hasn't been all sunshine and rainbows over the years, but we've tackled our problems and issues side by side." He pointed at her with his spoon. "So, if you and Aubry are 'just friends,' then I'm happy for you."

"Well said, honey." Her mother beamed at him. "Although your dad left out the most important part: God is an integral member of our marriage. He keeps us on track better than anything we could do ourselves."

"I've been praying about what to do." Estelle broke apart her roll, then laid the warm pieces on her plate. "I'm not sure what I expected, but things seem vastly different than before. More...intense." She shrugged. "I'm not sure that's the right word."

Her dad patted her arm. "As I said, he's seen and done things a man shouldn't have to, and it's changed him, so your relationship is different. Give him time, honey. No need to rush into marriage." When she opened her mouth to protest, he held up one hand. "I know, you may not be headed that way. Maybe he's the one, maybe not." He smirked. "But if he squirms as much as you do when questioned, it's real."

Estelle forced herself to sit still, then ate a spoonful of soup so she wouldn't have to answer.

Hands stuffed into his pockets, Aubry turned away from Estelle's house and limped down the street. His leg throbbed from his hip to his ankle, but with any luck, the ache in his limb would mask the shards of pain in his heart. Perspiration trickled down his spine and pooled under his arms. He frowned. With its heat and humidity, Maryland in August had to be one of the most miserable places on earth.

He sighted a bench ahead, his breath labored. Like it or not, he needed to rest before he went any farther. Foot scraping the sidewalk as it dragged, he trudged to the bench, then dropped onto the wooden seat with a grunt. Massaging his thigh, he closed his eyes and bowed his head.

Other than the rumble of an occasional car, the tree-lined street was quiet. Most people would be sitting down for dinner, while the poor souls working at the factories would toil for another couple of hours before the end of their shift. Fed up with the war, he hadn't bothered to apply for jobs at the manufacturing plants, so he couldn't complain that he hadn't found employment.

What did it matter if he had a job? Estelle made it clear that friendship was the extent of her interest. Hadn't electricity coursed through her extremities when they'd kissed? She'd felt something. She'd melted into his embrace, her arms twining around his waist, her lips softening under his. Had she never been kissed? Did her desire stem from the novelty of the act?

The bristles of his beard rough under his fingers, he rubbed his jaw, then froze. Had she been disgusted by his facial hair? He'd been clean shaven before he left.

Footsteps sounded. He raised his chin and cracked his eyelids. A dark-haired woman wearing a Kelly-green dress approached. His shoulders stiffened. Had she followed him? Been watching while he escorted Estelle home?

He pressed his lips together as she lowered herself beside him. Crossing his arms, he lifted the eyebrow of his uncovered eye. Would she get the message?

"Aubry. How've you been?" Her voice held no vestiges of warmth.

"Let's get right to the point and dispense with the fake pleasantries, shall we?"

"Goodness, what put you in such a vile mood?" Her eyes widened, and she shot him a smug smile. "Girl troubles?"

"Leave Estelle out of this." He inched away from her. "What do you want?"

"As if you didn't know."

"Spell it out for me." He glanced to the right. The street remained empty. The woman was bolder than usual being seen in the open wearing bright-green attire. Was the idea to hide in plain sight? Would Estelle get wind of the meeting from some nosy neighbor peeking through their curtains?

"Relax. This is a bus stop. Two people seated on this bench is normal."

"You've done your homework."

"Surprised?"

"No, now get on with it, then leave me alone."

"She really did put you in a foul mood."

He started to climb to his feet. "I don't need to listen to this."

She tugged his arm, and he glared at her hand, then her face. Her sneer faltered, and she released him, lacing her fingers in her lap.

"There's no need to be adversarial."

"I'll be the judge of that."

"All right. Enough. We've given you time to get settled. It's time to serve your government."

Gesturing to his patch, Aubry snarled, "Again. Serve them again. I told you, I already did my part."

"And your country thanks you, but the job isn't finished. We need your help, or we wouldn't be asking.

Aubry swallowed a smile. She actually had the decency to look abashed. Maybe the woman had a soul after all. He pulled on his cuffs, then brushed unseen lint from his slacks. "One job. I'll do this one job, and then you'll leave me alone."

"But—"

"My answer is nonnegotiable. I've risked enough for my country, and you can't make me feel bad. I deserve a life, such as it is. Or at least a chance at a normal life. Clear?"

She nodded. "Clear."

He swiveled his neck to stare at her. "Have you ever been in love?"

A shadow crossed her face, but she didn't answer.

"Ah, you lost him. I'm sorry. But that means you understand. And now that I'm home safe, I want to stay that way."

"Nothing is guaranteed, Mr. DeLuca. You could get hit by a car."

"Perhaps, but at least I have some level of control over that. With your gig, not so much. Now, what do I have to do?" He wanted a job, but risking his life for the government wasn't what he had in mind. Would he return from battle only to die at home?

CHAPTER TWENTY-ONE

Estelle checked her appearance in the mirror one last time. Tinged deep pink, there was no need to pinch her cheeks for color. Humidity had made her hair nearly unmanageable, and it had taken twice as long to wrestle her locks into victory rolls. She'd almost pulled the unruly tresses into a bun at the base of her neck, but that was both unflattering and too cliché as a librarian. She'd put on her favorite red dress, but it had done little to calm her nerves. Between the anticipation of seeing Aubry and the knowledge that the success of the book sale rested on her, she was as jumpy as a cat in a room full of rocking chairs.

She wagged her finger at the reflection. "Stop worrying. There's nothing you can do about either one at this point."

"Did you say something, dear?" Her mother's voice was muffled outside the door.

"Just talking to myself." Estelle whirled away from the mirror, then opened the door. "A tad nervous this morning. I want everything to go well."

"I'd be surprised if you weren't mobbed. Folks have been talking about the sale for the last three days, everywhere I've been." She patted Estelle's shoulder. "Breakfast is ready."

"Thanks for the encouragement. As for the offer for food, I'm too jittery to eat."

Her mother smiled. "I thought that might be the case, so I packed you a bag. It's on the counter."

Giving her mother a quick hug, Estelle blinked back tears. What was wrong with her? She was never much of a crier, and now her eyes filled at the smallest provocation. "You're the best. I'll see you tonight."

"Oh, no. Your father and I will be there during his lunch hour." Her mother winked. "Hopefully, all the good stuff won't be gone."

"Not a chance." Estelle grinned, then hurried down the steps and into the kitchen where she grabbed the canvas bag from the counter. The sack was heavy, so she peeked inside. Her mother had packed food for breakfast, lunch, and several snacks. If Estelle ever got an appetite, there would plenty to eat.

Heels clicking on the floor, she headed for the front door, which her mother had already opened. Beaming, she jerked her head outside. "You've got an escort this morning."

Breathless, Estelle peered through the screen. Aubry stood at the end of the walkway, hat in hand. Wearing a light-gray suit, offset with a white shirt and charcoal-colored tie, he was more handsome than usual. Or was that her imagination? "Oh. Well..."

"Relax, honey. Just take each moment as it comes." Estelle's mother swung open the screen door. "I'll be praying for the two of you and the success of the fair. Try to have fun."

With a nod, Estelle slipped outside and waved at Aubry. Heart in her throat, she swallowed and tried to look nonchalant. "Good morning. Did I miss something? I didn't know you were coming."

"Last-minute decision. I woke early, so here I am." He put his hat on, then tugged at the brim, setting the fedora at an angle and giving him a roguish appearance. "Guess I'm more invested in the sale than I thought." He cleared his throat, and his gaze seemed to caress her. "You look lovely, Estelle. Red suits you. Let me carry your bag."

"Thanks." Her face burned as she handed him the canvas sack. They set off down the street. Why did she have to blush at the slight compliment? "You're not bad yourself. You didn't need to wear a suit. It's not a formal event."

"I was hoping to impress your customers. Little old ladies love a man in a suit."

She snorted a laugh, and her face warmed even more. How ladylike. "Shame on you. Playing with their emotions."

He gave her a saucy smile. "Just doing my bit for the war effort."

"You're incorrigible."

With a shrug, he crooked his arm. "With any luck, that's the way you like your men."

Gasping, she hesitated for a moment, then slipped her hand into the bend of his elbow. She'd never seen him this flirtatious. What had gotten into him? She was pleased that he seemed to have shed much of his anger and darkness, but this new side of him confused her. And drew her.

They walked the last few blocks to the library in silence except for a couple of times when he'd pointed out a garden that was exceptionally pretty. Since when did he notice flowers? What had happened to him since yesterday?

At the entrance to the library, she withdrew her hand, dug into her purse for her keys, and unlocked the door. She led Aubry inside, then shivered when he placed his hand on the small of her back.

His forehead wrinkled. "You can't possibly be cold."

She nibbled on her lower lip. What to say? His touch sent a thrill up her spine? A snicker escaped.

"Anything you want to share?"

"Not particularly." She shrugged, a smile tugging at her mouth. "Every woman has her secrets."

"Hm. I'm not sure if I should be intrigued or frightened."

"Probably both."

His chuckle followed her down the hall. She ducked into the break room where she stowed her purse. Smoothing her skirts, she hurried to the storeroom. Devoid of his jacket, and sleeves rolled up, he was already pulling out boxes. He gestured to the bag of bundled books. "You can grab that, then cloth the tables and arrange the volumes as I deliver them. After I get finished, I'll give you a hand."

"Sounds good." She picked up the bag, then walked beside him as he made the first trip with a box. The muscles in his forearms bunched with the effort, and she forced her gaze away. Then he bent to put down the load, and the muscles in his back strained against his shirt. Her mouth dried, and she gave herself a mental slap. It was going to be a long day.

Aubry turned and went back to the closet. She fanned herself with one hand, and the heat on her face had nothing to do with the summer temperatures. Taking a deep breath, she unfolded the cloths and covered the tables, then began to set out the books and bundles. A short time later, Francine arrived with a cheery wave and headed to the circulation desk.

Thirty minutes later, the display was complete, and it was time to open the library. Estelle went to the entrance and gaped through the window. Dozens of people stood in line waiting to get in. She fumbled with the key, unlocked the knob, then opened the door. Men, women, and children surged past her.

Minutes blurred into hours as the books seemed to fly off the tables. Her parents arrived at lunchtime, but she was too busy to do more than point to the history and biography sections, their favorites. Aubry kept up a steady stream of conversation with patrons, making recommendations for purchases. Her stomach rumbled, but stopping to eat wasn't an option.

They moved back and forth behind the tables, in what felt like a well-choreographed dance, only bumping occasionally. His fingers would lightly touch her arm, shoulder, or back, indicating which direction to move. Their eyes met periodically, sending messages of amusement or irritation about a particular customer.

Her feet ached, but how much more did Aubry's leg hurt? His limp was more pronounced than when he arrived, but his jaw wasn't tight like usual when he was in pain. What a trooper.

He winked, and her pulse raced. Did he know how much she'd begun to care for him?

CHAPTER TWENTY-TWO

Aubry stretched his arms over his head and rotated his neck as Estelle ushered the last two patrons out the door, then locked the building. He ran his fingers through his hair. They'd been moving nonstop all day. The sale was a rousing success with only a dozen or so books remaining on the table. Reminiscent of a cocktail party, the library had buzzed with conversation and laughter as people perused titles and discussed their friends' choices. The only sound missing was clinking glasses.

Mrs. Ryskamp clapped her hands. "Well done, everyone! Thank you for your hard work."

Francine beamed. "Estelle and I can count the money, if you'd like to go home, Mrs. Ryskamp."

"I should stay."

"Nonsense." Estelle shook her head. "There's not much left to do. Besides, you're opening tomorrow."

"Well, if you insist. I wouldn't mind getting home earlier than I'd planned."

Francine handed the director her pocketbook. "I'll call you with the final tally, so you don't have to wait until morning to find out."

"Perfect." She sighed. "I might be getting too old for this."

"Not even close." Aubry shook his head. "Do you have a ride, or would you like me to call Mom to come get you?"

"I've got the car." Fatigue lined her face. "Thanks, Aubry."

She lifted her hand in a tired gesture, then headed out the door. Estelle locked it behind her.

He massaged his thigh that should hurt more than it did from being on his feet all day. Maybe the docs were wrong when they told him he'd experience aches and pain in the leg for the rest of his life. *Are You healing me completely, Lord?*

Estelle walked to the table, her eyes shining. "I can't believe we almost sold out."

"And you were nervous about the event." He smiled. "I hate to be an 'I told you so,' but I told you so."

She snickered. "Next time I'll listen to you."

"I doubt it, but thanks for saying." He grinned as he bent to grab an empty box from under the table, then piled the leftover books into the carton. "I'll put this in the closet. What else needs to be done?"

"Francine and I will count the money, if you'll stack the empty boxes in the closet. The tablecloths can go on one of the shelves in there, too." She cocked her head. "Do you mind? We can finish up, if you'd like to go home."

"Nope, I'm in it until the bitter end."

"Thanks." She blew out a loud breath, her face pale. "I'm bushed."

"Happy to help." He motioned toward the circulation desk where Francine waited. "Go sit down."

With a nod, she trudged toward the desk, her shoulders slumped. His heart tugged at her obvious fatigue. She'd worked hard today, never once stopping for food or a break. An image invaded his mind of her lying on his mother's sofa, a cool compress on her forehead while he rubbed her slender feet with his hands. The vision faded, but his pulse skittered. "Get a grip, man." He hoisted the box into his arms and headed for the closet.

The day had been the best he'd had since coming home. He hadn't once thought about his injuries or the war. No one seemed to stare at his patch or act repulsed. Many had expressed joy at his safe return, then spoke highly of his mother. Quite a few customers asked his opinion about titles, and he'd gladly shared what he knew about the books. Even stingy Mr. Walters had purchased a couple of volumes. More than a few folks had intimated how happy they were to see Estelle and him together, but he'd said nothing to confirm or deny their unspoken questions.

Then there'd been the amount of time he'd been able to spend in close proximity to Estelle, often close enough to catch the smell of soap on her hair or the rosewater on her skin. The temperature in the library had gone from stuffy to stifling by lunchtime, then nearly suffocating by midafternoon. Yet she looked as fresh as when he'd picked her up this morning. Did she have any idea how beautiful she was?

He stripped the tablecloths from the tables, then folded and tucked them into an empty space on one of the shelves. Satisfied he'd put away everything, he sauntered to the front desk.

"How's our honorary librarian?" Estelle smirked. "Finish your job?"

With an exaggerated bow, he said, "Ma'am, yes ma'am."

Francine laughed, and Estelle's smile broadened.

"It wouldn't be the worst thing I've been called." He wagged his index finger at her. "Are you talking about me so I won't remember your birthday?"

Her cheeks flamed. "No."

"Right." He winked at Francine. "Did you know our girl's birthday is coming up? How old will you be, Miss Johnson?"

"Never ask a woman's age." Francine swatted at him, but the look of interest on her face told of her desire to know the answer." Shame on you."

He guffawed. "My apologies."

Estelle rubbed at a spot on the counter. "You probably won't believe me, but I was going to invite you and your mom over next

Saturday. Mother wants to combine my birthday celebration with a homecoming for you.”

His stomach clenched. “A crowd?”

“Just us.”

“Ah, okay.” His breath eased out. “I’ll ask Mom.”

“You kids head on out.” Francine motioned toward the door. “I’ll call Mrs. Ryskamp with the total, then leave.”

“Are you sure, Francine?” Estelle said. “We can wait.”

The librarian shook her head. “No need, but thanks.”

“Okay, See you tomorrow.”

With an absentminded wave, Francine turned to the telephone and picked up the receiver.

Aubry draped his suit coat over his arm, then bowed. “After you, birthday girl.”

She rolled her eyes but looked pleased as they walked outside into the late-afternoon sunshine. The heat still clung to the air, and Aubry groaned. “Come on, fall.”

With a sidelong glance, she said, “Don’t wish our lives away.”

“No, but these temperatures are about kill me.”

“It is miserable.” She nodded. “I told Mother not to go to a lot of trouble for the party, but she insists. Says a girl only turns thirty once, as if that's a big deal. Frankly, it feels wrong to be celebrating while the war is still going on."

"With rationing still in effect, it won't be that big a deal." He pulled her hand into the bend of his elbow. "But there's no reason to feel guilty. The war is important, but if we let it rob us of even a little joy, the Nazis will have won. They want us to live in fear. We can't do that."

"True. A few weeks before you got home, Pastor Gibson preached about being thankful all year, not just at Thanksgiving. Thankful, in spite of our circumstances, rather than because of them."

"Mitch, the orderly you met, talks about that a lot. It used to bug me because I felt sorry for myself. And the other guys who'd been banged up, but he's right. If you see him again, don't tell him I said that."

She held up one hand as if taking an oath. "I promise." Squeezing his arm with her other hand, she snickered, her laugh tinkling like silver bells. "Thanks for all your help and walking me home."

"Absolutely. I'll always be there for you." His heart skipped. Did she understand what he was telling her?

CHAPTER TWENTY-THREE

The acrid smell of sulphur filled the air, and smoke wafted across the dinner table. Estelle sat back and huffed out a breath. "Good thing you didn't put all thirty candles on the cake."

"We couldn't get the fire permit." Aubry winked at her. "Although we tried."

Mrs. DeLuca looked horrified. "Aubry!"

Estelle laughed and waved her hand in a dismissive gesture. "Don't worry, Mrs. DeLuca, I'm not offended. Because no matter how old I am, he's always older. And he'll get his comeuppance. It's just a matter of time."

Her father picked up the knife and cut large squares of cake. "Of that, I have no doubt. Watch your back, Aubry."

"All the time, sir."

His mother stood and picked up the iced-tea pitcher, then made her way around the table, refilling glasses. "Enough of that, boys, or we'll banish you to the kitchen. Without your cake."

Aubry pressed a hand against his chest. "Harsh punishment." He leveled his gaze at Estelle. "It wouldn't be the same being alone."

Pulse skittering, Estelle ducked her head. He'd been making veiled comments all night. Had her parents or Mrs. DeLuca noticed? Was she reading meaning into his words?

"Hey, you'd have me." Estelle's father handed him a plate. "There's whipped cream in the bowl, son. Help yourself."

"Not exactly the company I'm looking for."

Her father chuckled. "No, I suppose not." He passed the remaining slices of cake, then picked up his fork. "How are things going on the job hunt? I'd have thought you'd have been snapped up by now."

"Slow. Not that I want to work the line at one of the factories, but I can't see well enough to do the work, and I have no desire to count their profits. I'd like to land in a bank or investment house. I only have a handful of years' experience."

"Surely your war service means something."

Aubry shrugged. "Not in the finance industry. Shooting at Germans is hardly a transferrable skill."

"I meant your leadership skills. You were a captain."

Estelle nibbled on her cake and watched the exchange. Aubry's bitterness and anger seemed to have been replaced with a clinical detachment. Was that healthy? Should she try to find Mitch and ask? Did she have a right to the information? Her stomach suddenly felt like a rock, and she set down her fork.

A week had passed since the book sale, and she hadn't seen him since then. She'd gone over twice to read, but he'd been out, and his mother had no idea where he'd gone. What was he hiding? Was he avoiding her? He'd been warm and friendly, and more than a little solicitous since arriving tonight. Was she jumping at shadows and inferring things that weren't there?

"I must have this recipe, Norma." Mrs. DeLuca poked at the cake. "This is some of the best gingerbread I've ever had."

"Sure. It's from Lola Wyman's *Better Meals in Wartime.* It only takes a half cup of sugar and one egg. I'll let you borrow the book. We've found several new favorites."

"Wonderful, thank you."

Her mother patted Estelle's shoulder. "Hopefully, next year we'll be able to make you a real cake with frosting on top."

"The Allies are making progress in Europe." Estelle's father poked the air with his finger. "You may be closer to the truth than you realize. The boys have Hitler and his Jerries on the run."

"Vern, you promised there'd be no war talk tonight."

"Right. Sorry." Not looking the least bit abashed, Vern carved a bite of cake from his slice. "Let's tell stories about the birthday girl, and see if we can embarrass her."

"Or not." Estelle made a face at him. "We could hurry up and eat so I can open presents."

He snapped his fingers. "Presents? I knew I forgot something."

Aubry snorted a laugh. "Yeah, we didn't get the word about gifts, either."

"Oh, you men." Her mother rolled her eyes, then shot him a wicked smile. "Fortunately for you, Vern, I took care of things, and you'll be happy to know you were very generous. Now, finish your cake, and we'll have coffee and *presents* in the living room."

Her father chuckled. "I'm glad to know I'm such a thoughtful guy. I can't wait to see what I got you."

The tightness eased from Estelle's chest, and she picked up her fork. Her dad always lightened her mood, even when he didn't know she needed cheering up. His sense of humor was often dry, but he also used razor-sharp sarcasm on occasion. Tonight, he'd pulled her into a warm embrace and whispered how proud he was of her. Not a demonstrative man with kisses or hugs, the gesture meant more than any material gift. She giggled. Me, too."

Moments later, they'd eaten their fill. Her mother pushed back her chair and stood. "Estelle and I will clear the table and make the coffee. You can head into the living room.

Mrs. DeLuca picked up her plate and got up. "Nonsense. I'll help, and you'll give me no argument. We're friends, not guests."

"Thank you." Estelle's mother smiled. "The work will go faster."

Her father clapped Aubry on the back. "Looks like it's just you and me, son."

Estelle caught the look of panic that swept across Aubry's face before he schooled his features. Had her father caught his expression? What did Aubry think they were going to discuss?

"Stop woolgathering, Estelle." Her mother beckoned her toward the kitchen. "Irene will handle the coffee, so you can clear the table, then dry the dishes after I wash them."

She jerked her head toward her mother and stuttered, "O-of course." She stacked the empty cake plates as Aubry and her father disappeared down the hall. What did men talk about? She went into the kitchen and slipped the cake into the icebox, then set the plates on the counter, next to the sink. Making several trips, she quickly moved the soiled dishes to the kitchen.

The coffee had been percolating during dinner, and its rich, nutty flavor filled the small room. Mrs. DeLuca pulled one of Estelle's mother's trays from the cupboard and arranged five cups and saucers next to a small pitcher of milk. She scooped the dinner leftovers into smaller bowls, then wrapped them in waxed paper. Estelle retrieved a couple of towels from the drawer by the stove and began to dry the dishes.

Her mother plunged her hands into the soapy water. "This was such a lovely evening. It's nice to see you and Aubry courting again. Don't you agree, Irene?"

"Absolutely."

"We're not courting." Estelle tightened her grip on the plate. "We're just friends. Well, maybe more than that, but we're just trying to get reacquainted, to see where things go."

"That's what courting is, dear." Mrs. DeLuca turned from the icebox. "At least, that's what it was like when I was a girl. But no matter. Whatever it is, you're helping him heal, and for that, I'm grateful."

"He does seem to be recovering." Estelle put the plate on top of the others she'd dried. "But I'm sure it's God, not me. I've been praying."

"For it is God which worketh in you, both to will and to do of His good pleasure." Mrs. DeLuca closed the icebox. "We're His hands and feet, child. Don't sell yourself short."

"Well said, Irene." Estelle's mother drained the sink, then picked up the second towel. "Why don't you take the tray in to your father and Aubry. Irene and I will be in momentarily."

Estelle sent the two women a sly smile. "So you two can talk about me?"

"A mother's privilege."

With a laugh, Estelle picked up the tray and headed out of the kitchen, her ears straining to hear what they had to say, but silence reigned. Her mother was smart enough to wait until Estelle was out of earshot. As she strolled down the hall, her father's bass voice floated toward her.

"I know Estelle's of age and has a right to do what she wishes, but I'd like to know what your intentions are, Aubry."

Swallowing a gasp, Estelle froze, her palms moist against the silver tray.

"I love her, sir. I'd like to ask her to be my wife, but she deserves better than me, half a man."

"Ridiculous. Just because you're scarred doesn't make you half a man. It's what's on the inside."

"Well, to be honest, I'm struggling with that, too. I don't understand why God would do this to me."

"He didn't do it to you, but He may have allowed it. His ways are confusing, to be sure. You may never know exactly why He let you be injured in such a way, but at a minimum, He will use the experience to grow your faith in Him and His sovereignty."

"Yes, sir."

"Not an easy lesson. Take it from me."

"Sir?"

"I was in the last war. Estelle was two years old when I decided to enlist."

She had no right to eavesdrop further, so she cleared her throat and walked heavily to warn them of her arrival. Knowing her inability to hide her emotions, she avoided Aubry's questioning gaze as she entered the room. He'd said he loved her and wanted to propose. Was that true, or did he think, from her father's tone, that's what he wanted to hear? Did she want to know the answer?

CHAPTER TWENTY-FOUR

Laurel's streets were deserted as Aubry strolled the sidewalks downtown. Dusk was giving way to inky skies as the night had finally arrived for him to fulfill his agreement with the mysterious woman from the OSS. She'd finally given him the name of the organization, but before committing himself, he'd made her prove her relationship to the agency that was the worst-kept secret in Washington. She'd been miffed at his lack of trust, but he'd reminded her that anyone could claim to be helping the US win the war, when in reality be an enemy agent. He ground his teeth at her arrogant assumption that he would kowtow to her wishes after seeing an identity card that could easily have been forged. How naïve did she think he was?

Rather than be seen together, she'd given him instructions on where to find the organization's headquarters in a collection of buildings not far from the marbled Lincoln Memorial. What would the venerable president think about the current war? The Civil War had torn apart a country, but the current conflict had threatened to tear apart the world.

The train trip from Laurel to the nation's capital had been uneventful, but he found himself studying his fellow passengers. What were their stories? Was anyone headed to his destination? All dressed in somber business suits, none were on a pleasure trip. But to a person, every man kept his eyes averted. What was that all about?

Keeping knowledge of his journey from Estelle had been difficult, and he winced at the memory of their last conversation. He'd led her to believe he was seeing a doctor at Meade, and she offered to accompany him. Assuring her the appointment was a simple follow-up, and that he'd be fine, he wondered if he should have claimed a job interview. Either way, she'd want to know the outcome. With a sigh, he massaged the back of his neck. Muscles tight, they barely moved under his fingers.

He was sure she'd see through his subterfuge, but apparently, he was a better liar than he'd thought. Or hoped to be. Not a skill he wanted to develop. How did career spies keep from forgetting the web of deceit they wove—from losing their mind?

He'd met with the woman's superior, a short, ugly man of indeterminate age. He, too, had been peeved that Aubry wanted proof of their existence. A week had passed since the interchange, and now he was creeping around Laurel to do their bidding.

A crash sounded down one of the alleys, and his heart banged in his chest. He pivoted as a white cat shot out from between the buildings, racing across the macadam as if the animal had seen a ghost. Aubry let out a ragged breath, then chuckled. He was definitely not cut out for spy stuff. He wasn't a coward, but a lifetime of creeping around wasn't for him.

Darkness had descended in full over the town, and thanks to continued blackout regulations and a new moon, he was invisible, even to someone with twenty-twenty vision. He slipped behind the three-story clapboard house that had been converted to offices. Was anyone inside? Blackout curtains made it impossible to know. Warned that he was on his own if caught, he sent a prayer heavenward for safety.

Was it fair to ask God's help? Aubry's assignment was supposedly for the greater good of the county. Did that make his actions right? Would he live to regret his agreement?

Enough ruminating.

He ducked behind the building, ears straining to pick up the slightest indication that he wasn't alone. Fortunately, an unexpected result of his diminished vision was the sharpening of his hearing. Mouth slightly open as he'd been taught in the army, he focused on the noises carried by the gentle breeze: the rustling of the leaves in the branches overhead, the squeak of a bat, and the buzz of a mosquito. As he walked, he lifted each leg higher than normal and shortened his steps, then placed his foot on the ground, holding back his weight to test the landing spot. Who knew combat skills would be necessary in downtown Laurel?

Arriving at the back door of his target house, Aubry glanced left, then right. He pulled the key from his pocket, trying not to think what the OSS had done to obtain a copy, and let himself inside, the lock giving a slight *snick* as the tumbler released. He froze, again listening for signs of other inhabitants. Nothing. Running his hands along the wall to guide his journey, he counted doorways. Second one on the left, according to the woman. He wrapped his fingers around the knob, and his eyes widened. Unlocked. Was someone behind the door?

He held his breath and put his ear near the wood, then closed his eyes. Seconds passed. Nothing. He released his pent-up breath, then opened the door and slipped into the room. Arms outstretched, he crept across the room and checked the windows to ensure the curtains had been pulled. He clicked on his flashlight, then swept the beam back and forth to get the lay of the room. He'd been given a diagram, but if he'd learned anything overseas, it was to never assume he had all the information he needed or that the information was accurate.

The office was sparse with a single desk in the center, a bookshelf on one wall, and three wooden filing cabinets against the other. The desktop was empty, save for a telephone and a small lamp. Listing to the right, the chair had seen better days. He moved toward the cabinets, and the floor creaked. He stilled for a moment, then inched forward.

In front of the cabinets, he fumbled in his pocket for the key, then unlocked the middle cabinet with a muted *thunk*. He slid open the drawer, then leaned close to the files and rifled through each one, labeled in large block print, as if they knew a blindman was coming. Could his subject make the task any easier?

Aubry spied the folder he needed, pulled it out, and laid it on the desk, then turned on the lamp and tilted the shade to illuminate the pages. A brief perusal of the file didn't reveal anything unusual. It appeared to be a legitimate collection of memos, letters, and invoices. He slipped the small camera he'd been issued, from his pocket, then snapped multiple pictures of each item. He did not want to come back.

Pulse tripping, he returned the folder and locked the cabinet. He turned off the light, put the camera in his pocket, then went to the door. Clicking off the flashlight, he cracked the door. Silence. Fighting the urge to scurry from the building like a squirrel with its tail on fire, he tiptoed down the hall.

Once outside the house, he set off down the street, forcing his gait to a leisurely stroll. After several blocks, his heart rate finally slowed to normal, but perspiration slithered down his back and trickled down the sides of his face. He wiped his moist hands on his trousers, then swallowed a sigh. He was definitely not cut out for clandestine work. But he'd held up his end of the bargain, and he was done.

Thirty minutes later, he arrived home, having eluded civil defense air raid wardens and plane spotters. The hair on the back of his neck prickled, and he whirled. A figure emerged from behind a tree, and he stiffened, a frown twisted his lips. The agreement had been to meet tomorrow. "Don't trust me, do you," he hissed.

"Plans changed. We need the photos tonight." The woman held out her hand. "That's all you need to know."

"Fine." He withdrew the camera from his pocket and slapped it into her hand, smiling to himself when she grunted at the force of the action. He was being petty, but he didn't care. "Now, we're square. Don't ever contact me again."

"Your country thanks you."

"Yeah, sure." He stalked toward the house. It was too late to do so, but he had the distinct desire to take a bath.

Chapter Twenty-Five

Pocketbook in hand, Estelle sauntered along the sidewalk toward town. Foot traffic was heavy on the way to the Labor Day celebration, but she was in no hurry since she'd started out early in order to stop at the library to pick up the book she'd left on Saturday. The rumble of voices mingled with laughter surrounded her, and the air crackled with joy.

Snippets of conversation about glowing newspaper reports floated past. The Allies had won several victories in the last ten days, the most recent of which was the retaking of Paris. Germany was on the run, and it was only a matter of time before a final victory was achieved. Perhaps by the new year. What would 1945 bring?

Estelle let the crowd sweep her along, and she was soon in front of the library. Extricating herself from the throng, she hurried up the walk, unlocked the door, and stepped inside. Her heels clicked on the wooden floor as she made her way to the desk. Closed up since Saturday, the building was stuffy and hot, amplifying the odor of old books and furniture polish.

Running a finger along the gleaming surface of the circulation counter, she smiled. Few places on earth made her as happy as the library. Her favorite task was to repair the books, especially older books that had seen much handling and love. She had to school herself not to get lost in the pages of whichever volume she was restoring. Of course, she enjoyed shelving the books, too, because then she could discover treasures she'd yet to read.

Both her parents were avid readers, so she came by her fascination of books early. Estelle's mother had probably read to her before she was born. Dinner-table talk centered around books more often than not, and she'd been surprised not to experience the same thing at her friends' homes.

She ducked under the counter and retrieved the book, then slipped it into her purse. Tempted to check the book drop, she shook her head. They and plenty more would be in the box tomorrow. Did others love their jobs as much as she did? She couldn't imagine working anywhere else. Most of her friends had applied at the factories or Fort Meade, making exorbitant salaries paid by the defense industry. But living at home meant her expenses were low, so she didn't need the higher salary. She shuddered at the thought of being trapped in a massive room enveloped by constant banging and thundering of machinery. Working in a manufacturing plant was definitely not for her.

Behind her, the clock let out a muted chime, and she glanced at the watch on her bodice. If she didn't get a move on, she'd be late for the mayor's speech. Not that missing it would be any great loss, but her father was sure to have plenty to say about it, and she needed to be prepared to give her opinion. Estelle's mother rarely got involved in these sorts of debates, preferring to play referee instead.

Rounding the desk, she rushed outside, then locked the door, and merged with the crowd that had grown since she'd been in the library. Were they giving something away? Bodies pressed up against her, and she drew her pocketbook close to her chest. A few minutes later, she arrived at the town center.

Despite being September, the temperature still hovered in the eighties, with humidity that made her dress cling to her skin. She wandered to a copse of maple trees, and the shade dropped the heat by a few degrees. She surveyed the faces. Would Aubry come? She hadn't seen him since her birthday, and he hadn't called. Her stomach fluttered. Had he meant the declaration of love for her that he'd given to her father? His silence said no.

A bandstand stood in the middle of a grassy park with terraced sides filled with shrubs and flowers. The wrought-iron railings were long gone, but the wooden benches remained. A couple from church waved at her from the top of one of the tiers, and she returned the gesture, a wide smile on her face. She threaded her way through the crowd toward the elderly couple, then froze.

With his back to her, Aubry was tucked deep in the corner of one of the tiers. She couldn't see his face, but she recognized his form, the slope of his shoulders, and uneven stance. His arms flailed as he talked to someone, but his body blocked whoever it was. She craned her neck, then shifted to the side. Still blocked. Huffing out a breath, she pushed forward. As she did, Aubry moved to the side revealing the mysterious woman she'd seen him with several weeks ago.

Dressed to the nines, the woman wore a bright-cobalt-blue dress that shimmered in the sunlight. Silk? Her straw hat bore flowers and a ribbon the same vibrant blue. A riot of raven-black hair framed her face as she smiled and put one hand on his shoulder.

Estelle's jaw dropped. Who was she? How could Aubry tell her father he loved Estelle when this woman obviously meant something to him. What sort of game was he playing?

Nausea swept over her. She pressed a hand against her middle. Had he been playing her all along? Her head snapped left, then right. She had to get out of here. Now.

Shoving past a pair of children, Estelle bumped into a middle-aged man who scowled at her. She mumbled an apology as she continued to push through the mob. She made it to the sidewalk that was mostly clear. Her vision blurred with tears, and she stumbled in the direction of home. A door opened to her left, and Mrs. Feeney emerged.

"Estelle?"

Her heart told her to keep moving, but her head said to stay. Her mother and father would be appalled if she ignored the elderly couple. She squared her shoulders and blinked away the moisture in her eyes, then forced a smile. "Hello. Nice to see you."

"Is everything all right, child?" Mrs. Feeney's forehead wrinkled. "You look distraught."

"I'm fine."

"I beg to differ, but I won't pry."

Estelle glanced at Mr. Feeney, and he kissed his wife's cheek. "I'll be next door when you're finished. He touched the brim of his hat and wandered away.

"He didn't have to leave."

"Yes, he did." Mrs. Feeney gestured to a bench a few yards away. "Let's sit for a moment."

"Okay." Estelle's chin trembled, and she pressed her lips together as she sat down next to her friend.

Mrs. Feeney patted her leg. "As I said, I won't pry, but you do seem upset, so I'd like to pray with you. Just to ask our Good Father for His help."

"It's Aubry." Estelle sniffled, and then she spelled out what had happened with the mysterious woman, and Aubry's declaration of love. When the torrent of words finally ceased, she sighed. "I think he's seeing another woman."

"Jumping to conclusions is a dangerous habit. You should ask him."

"I don't know."

"Keeping secrets and not dealing with issues isn't good for a healthy relationship, whether friendship or more. If you're not willing to speak to Aubry, you must at least pray about the situation. Ask God for wisdom and clarity." She pierced Estelle with a serious gaze. "But you must consider addressing this. Sooner rather than later. Trust me when I say, it won't get any better with time. In fact, quite the opposite."

Estelle squirmed and clenched her hands together in her lap. Would God tell her what was going on? Did she want to know?

CHAPTER TWENTY-SIX

The sun had barely crested the horizon, but Estelle swung her feet over the side of the bed. Eyes burning with grit, she yawned widely. Temperatures were still sweltering, and her nightgown clung to her form. She'd spent most of the night alternately praying and wrestling with the sheets, yet had found no solution. For whatever His reasons, God was silent on what she needed to do about Aubry.

Why hadn't He spoken to her? Did He expect her to work things out on her own? Was there some unforgiven sin blocking her path to her Heavenly Father?

With a sigh, she tiptoed down the hallway to the bathroom where she dampened a washcloth with cold water and blotted her face. The coolness soothed her hot skin, and she repeated the process several times. She brushed her teeth, then combed her hair before plaiting it into a single braid. Fortunately, she had the day off—the next two, actually—so she didn't have to interact with anyone but her folks if she didn't want to. And she didn't. The book sale had been incredibly successful, but she'd seen more people in eight hours than she'd seen in the last two weeks. She'd caught her limit.

She wandered back to her room and dragged on a cotton skirt and blouse, then poked her feet into the sandals she'd kicked off the night before. She made her bed, then padded around the room, and set things right. The tidier her room became, the calmer she felt. A place for everything, and everything in its place, as her grandmother used to say in a singsong voice. Task finished, she headed downstairs and through the semidark house.

Pink-and-purple fingers streaked the morning sky, and images began to take shape outside the window. Movement caught her eye, and she squinted through the glass. Mr. Levinson walking his dog, a small Boston terrier whose perky gait told of his excitement at being out. Oh, that life was as simple as a dog's life.

Forgive me, Lord. I'm being ungrateful. I just don't know what You want me to do. It's tempting to rush ahead on my own and hope You'll keep up, but it's just as tantalizing to run away from my problems. Go somewhere and start over. I was going to take things slow. Get reacquainted with Aubry and see where things went, but I've fallenl in love with him. What if he doesn't feel the same way about me? What if his words to Daddy were a farce, and he is enamored with this mystery woman?

Estelle prowled the room, straightening the stack of books on the coffee table, then folding the newspaper her father had left next to the rocker. She dropped into the chair and peered through the panes. The room was stuffy, but she doubted opening the window would help. The day promised to be another scorcher. And a long one.

Hours stretched before her. Estelle's mother had weeded the victory garden yesterday, and the house was spic-and-span as usual.

Estelle huffed out another sigh. Perhaps a stroll to the river was in order. She could dip her feet in the water and consider her options.

She scribbled a note for her folks, then hurried to the bedroom to grab her pocketbook before letting herself out of the house. Birds chattered in the branches overhead. Pink and purple gave way to blue as the sky brightened in the morning sun. Puffy white clouds materialized as she ambled down the street. The tightness in her chest seeped away as her feet ate up the distance to the riverbank.

As she crested the hill and looked down at the flowing water of the Patuxent, memories assailed her. Picnics with her parents. Splashing among the rocks with school chums. Ambling along the grassy berm and holding hands with Aubry. Thinking they had all the time in the world to get acquainted.

He'd been gone longer than they'd been together, yet the few weeks since his return somehow seemed richer, deeper, and more meaningful. The war was a harsh reminder that each day was a gift and never guaranteed.

Estelle slipped off her sandals, parked them and her purse next to an azalea bush, its blooms long gone, then headed down to the riverside. Bunching her skirt in one hand, she dipped one toe into the water. Not quite as warm as last night's bath, but cool enough to refresh. She stood for several minutes, letting her gaze ricochet along the tree line. Leaves fluttered in the hot breeze that carried overtones of soil mingled with factory exhaust.

After several more minutes, she rubbed her forehead. The river had not worked its usual magic. Her mind still raced, and her muscles refused to uncoil. She climbed the incline, then wiped her feet on the grass before donning her sandals.

"Lord, I really could use a sign." She trudged toward town, head down as she walked.

"Miss Johnson, is that you?"

She started at the voice and looked up.

A uniformed postal carrier walked toward her, a broad smile on his face and a scarred brown leather satchel over his right shoulder.

"Yes?"

He waved an envelope at her as he approached. "I'm sorry. You probably have no idea who I am. Your house is on my route, and I'm on my way there now, but I saw you and thought you might like to get your letter now rather than wait." He chuckled. "I'm rambling. Bad habit."

"Are you allowed to do that? Give me a letter here, not at home?"

"In the wild, as it were?" He shrugged. "I won't tell if you won't."

"My lips are sealed." She took the envelope and glanced at the return address. "It's from my aunt. Thank you so much. Just the pick-me-up I need."

"Letters are like that, aren't they? A bright spot in another otherwise uneventful day." He tipped his hat. "You have yourself a nice afternoon, Miss Johnson."

"You, too. And thanks again."

"My pleasure."

With a quick motion, she tore open the flap and withdrew a single sheet of paper. Her eyes raked the page, and she grinned. A cheerful, chatty missive, the letter read like her aunt talked: broken, uneven sentences, and lots of exclamation points. "Is this Your sign, Father? I'd sure like to think it is. A day or two away might give me the distance I need. And Auntie Mabel is sure to have good advice. She's as close to You as Mrs. Feeney."

Would her aunt's input echo that of the older woman or take Estelle down another path?

CHAPTER TWENTY-SEVEN

"Help me get there in time, Lord." Aubry lengthened his stride as he hurried along the sidewalk toward the bus station, his breath ragged. "I don't know why Estelle is leaving, but it must have something to do with me, otherwise she would have told me about her trip. I've messed up somehow. Give me the opportunity to fix whatever this is."

He should have proposed the day after her father asked his intentions. The man had pierced him with a gaze so deep, he'd felt like one of the insects pinned to the board his high school science teacher had displayed. Even with Aubry's poor vision, he could see her father's expression: Hurt my daughter, and you'll rue the day.

How had he managed to bungle the relationship? They'd had so many precious moments, especially over the last ten days, when they seemed to be getting closer. Even when they were at odds, he felt the tug of her spirit.

Foot traffic increased as he got closer to the station. Men and women rushed toward the building, suitcases or satchels in hand. A stream of people surged from inside, more than a few wearing uniforms, and most saluted as they passed. Did they recognize him as one of their own, or was the gesture simply a habit?

His gaze raked the sea of faces. Where was she? Was she already gone? Her parents said she was on the ten-fifteen bus, and the hands of the giant clock on the outside of the station read exactly ten fifteen. His heart thundered in his chest. "I can't lose her."

"I beg your pardon?" A porter stood at Aubry's elbow. "Did you need something, sir?"

"Yes!" Aubry's breath caught. "I'm looking for the northbound bus going to Pennsylvania. Harrisburg, specifically."

"That bus is about to leave, son. You've got to hurry."

"Can you hold it for me? It's very important."

A smile broke out on the porter's face. "Someone special you're hopin' to see?"

"How'd you know?"

"I've been working for this line almost forty years. I recognize the look." He squeezed Aubry's shoulder. "You follow me as fast as you can, but I'll go ahead and keep them from leaving. We're gonna go through the building and out the other side. The bus you want is the third one on the right."

"Thank you."

The man slipped through the crowd like a fish in the Patuxent, Aubry close on his heels. He didn't plan to lose him. Bumped and jostled by the throng, he kept his gaze riveted to the uniformed back of the porter. Perspiration trickled down his spine and slicked his face. The temperature inside the building was no better despite two fans spinning overhead. The crowd dispersed, some people heading to the ticket windows while others exited the doors on the far side. Voices, laughter, and footsteps filled the cavernous room.

Glancing over his shoulder, the porter grinned. "You're doing great, son."

They burst outside, and the man veered right, then waved both arms as he made a beeline for one of the buses.

Aubry stumbled, and his leg twisted, sending needles of pain through his thigh. He gasped but kept moving. He couldn't let his injury get in the way. Limping forward, he arrived at the door to the bus. The porter was in deep conversation with the driver. Both men turned to look at him, and the driver said, "How can I help you, mister?"

"I need to speak to one of your passengers."

"Either they get off or you get on. Pick one. I can't hang around. I gotta schedule to keep."

"How much to get to the end of the line?"

The driver's eyebrows shot to his hairline. "Must be some kind of conversation you're gonna have." He named an amount.

Digging into his pocket, Aubry pulled out several bills and counted them. His stomach roiled. "I'm two dollars short."

"Close enough." The driver waved him on, then pulled out his wallet and extracted the money.

"I can't accept—"

"Of course you can." The porter gave him a gentle push from behind. "Anything for love, right, Otto?"

"Yep." The driver winked. "I can't wait any longer. I'm already five minutes late gettin' started."

Aubry shook the porter's hand, then climbed onto the bus and handed the driver his cash. "Thank you. I will pay you back."

With a smile, Otto shrugged and waved him toward the seats. He closed the door with a bang. "All aboard!"

Squinting, Aubry surveyed the faces in the bus, and his heart leapt. Estelle sat near the back of the bus with an empty seat beside her. *Lord? Is that You working things out?*

Their eyes met as he approached, and her face paled. "Aubry," she whispered. "What are you doing here?"

He sank into the seat next to her. "I had to see you, Estelle. Set things straight between us." He raked his fingers through his hair, then rubbed his hands on his trousers. "I love you, more than I ever thought possible."

"What? No." She held up her hands as if to push him away. "That's not possible."

Lacing his fingers with hers, he angled his body toward hers. "Please, hear me out. I've been fighting the feeling since I got home, but I can't imagine my life without you. I'm desperately, hopelessly, and completely in love with you." He swallowed the lump that had formed in his throat. "I don't deserve you. I'm a broken man with a bum leg and one eye that partially works, but I wonder if you can find it in your heart to love me, even if only a little."

Her eyes narrowed. "How can you say that when there's someone else?"

He bolted upright. "Who? What do you mean?"

"I've seen you with a woman. Twice, and each time, the two of you were having a very *cozy* conversation. She stood quite close to you. Touching you. You can't tell me there's nothing going on with her?"

"Cozy conversation with a woman?" Realization dawned, and he barked a harsh laugh. "It wasn't like it seemed. I can't tell you much. Perhaps after the war, but I doubt it. I pray you believe what I'm about to tell you."

Estelle's expression was shuttered. "Go on."

Leaning close to her, he pitched his voice low. "The woman you saw works for the government, one of the new war agencies. I was assigned a task…a mission. One that I can't tell you about. Not now, maybe never, but I'm done with them. She means nothing to me." He squeezed her hands. "Please believe me. You are the only one for me. I'm a better man because of you. Your faith in God, and your ability to be thankful in spite of our circumstances, not because of them, has opened my eyes to how shallow my own faith has been. I want to be a man you can trust to do what's best. I've got nothing to offer but love. I have no job, and I'm still living at home with Mom, but I've got some savings, and I know someone will hire me, eventually." He released her and rose, then stepped into the aisle and got down on one knee, his thigh protesting every move. He grunted and pushed away the pain. "Can you see your way clear to becoming my wife?"

Conversation on the bus had ceased, the only sound being the rumble of the engine. An air of expectation blanketed the vehicle.

Her hands flew to her throat as she gazed at him. Oh, if only his vision were better and he could see the emotions on her face. His mouth dried as he waited for her answer. Time stood still. Finally, when he could stand it no longer, she smiled and nodded. "I love you, too."

"And?"

"And I'll marry you."

Cheers and applause erupted as the bus driver honked the horn, and Aubry grinned. He hadn't planned to put on a show, but somehow sharing the moment with a bus full of strangers seemed right. He tried to stand, but his thigh cramped. He groaned, then someone's arm went around his shoulder, and another around his waist, helping him up, then into his seat. Beaming, a pair of burly men saluted, then returned to their own seats without a word.

"Are you sure? You just witnessed how defective I am."

She rested her hand on his chest. "But you're not defective in here, and that's what matters." She sent him a wicked smile. "Now, are you going to kiss me or not?"

His pulse raced as he drew her close, his face inches from hers. "If you insist."

"I do." She brushed her lips against his, gently like a feather.

He cupped her face in his hands and kissed her, the noise and chaos of the bus fading away as he lost himself in the taste of her.

EPILOGUE

November 23, 1944

The aroma of roasting chicken encompassed the house as Estelle ran up the stairs to get ready. She and her mother had been preparing the Thanksgiving meal since dawn. Aubry and Mrs. DeLuca would arrive soon, as would her father. He'd been called into work for some sort of emergency.

She hurried into her room and opened the closet door. They had much to be thankful for, the least of which was her wedding on Saturday. The Axis powers were losing ground, the Allies having liberated many occupied areas and broken through Germany's west wall. Even the Japanese were beginning to lag. Many newspapers speculated that the war might be over by next summer. She prayed daily that it would be sooner, so that fewer boys and men would die or be injured. "Bring them all home, God."

Standing in front of the closet, she rifled through her dresses. She'd initially thought to wear her navy crepe, but the color seemed too somber for the occasion. Her gaze fell on her mother's frothy white wedding gown that had been altered to fit Estelle. Silk shimmered under the lace overlay. The seamstress had changed the original puffed sleeves to more close fitting, but the high neck remained. The train had been kept the same, its six-foot length made her feel like a princess. She glanced at the dresser where the crown and veil lay waiting to be worn.

Her heart swelled, and tears pricked the backs of her eyes. In two days, she would be Mrs. Aubry DeLuca, a dream come true. Aubry had found a job at an investment firm in Baltimore, and they'd found a lovely home located minutes from the office by bus. After they'd informed his mother of their engagement, she'd surprised them with the news that she'd been holding the insurance money from Mr. DeLuca's death. The funds were enough to purchase the duplex home outright, and they insisted she take the other half.

Rationing was still in place, so the reception wouldn't be a large spread, but perhaps they could throw a party at war's end. Meanwhile, she had less than forty-eight hours left before she'd be walking the aisle. She smiled at the memory of her and Aubry announcing in unison that they wanted to marry over Thanksgiving weekend. They hadn't conferred on the date, so she knew it was meant to be.

"Stop woolgathering, girl. He'll be here any minute." She peeked into the closet and spied her burgundy dress. Perfect. Made of rayon, it was lightweight and looked silky without actually being silk. Affordable and more comfortable as far as she was concerned. The bodice was smocked, and tiny burgundy-colored beads were embedded among the folds of fabric. The cap sleeves were beaded, too.

Estelle pulled out the dress and held it up against herself, then walked to the full-length mirror and inspected her appearance. Twirling, she smiled as the skirt billowed. Yes, the burgundy was the right choice. She hurried to the bathroom to brush her teeth and take a spit bath as her mother called it. Finished with her ablutions, she went back to her room and slipped the dress over her head. With quick strokes, she pinned the front of her hair into victory rolls, and let the rest hang down her back in soft waves, the way Aubry preferred.

Her stomach quivered at the memory of his touch last night. He'd threaded his fingers through her tresses, sending shivers up her spine. His kiss before leaving had been more fervent than usual, and he'd murmured that the two days before the wedding would be the longest of his life.

The doorbell rang, and her breath caught. She'd been so lost in thought, she hadn't heard the car pull up in the driveway. Flushed with anticipation, she didn't need to pinch her cheeks for color. She poked her feet into her black pumps, dabbed on a bit of lipstick, then took a deep breath and yanked open the door. She forced herself to walk sedately down the stairs until she caught sight of Aubry through the side window.

Footsteps sounded, and her mother came down the hall and met her in the foyer. "I was just getting ready to call you. You look radiant." She winked. "Like a woman in love." Before Estelle could reply, she opened the door.

Aubry and Mrs. DeLuca stepped into the house, his mother enveloping Estelle in a warm embrace. "You look lovely, dear. Radiant, I'd say."

Estelle's mother burst into laughter. "I just told her the same thing, Irene. Can you tell she's in love?"

"All right, you two, stop embarrassing my bride-to-be." Aubry slipped an arm around her waist and pulled her close. "Do I look radiant? I'm in love, too."

Everyone chuckled, and her mother motioned toward the dining room. Her father appeared in the doorway, and Estelle blinked. She hadn't heard him arrive, either. Would love make her this addled about everything?

China, crystal, and silverware gleamed in the midday sunlight that streamed through the windows. Her grandmother's silver, three-armed candelabra graced the center of the table, pine greens nestled at the candleholder's base. In the time she'd been upstairs, her mother had filled the table with serving bowls and platters of food.

Estelle's father rubbed his hands together and stepped back. "Welcome! What a blessing to spend this day together. Have a seat, and let the celebration begin. We have much to be grateful for this year."

Mrs. DeLuca beamed. "Amen to that."

They sat down, and Estelle's father held out his hands, and Estelle grasped his fingers. Aubry took her other hand, his grip firm yet gentle. He stroked the back of her hand with his thumb, and a jolt of electricity shot to her shoulder. She peeked at him out of the corner of her eye and swallowed a giggle. His smirk said he knew how his touch affected her.

Estelle bowed her head as her father prayed, "Dear Heavenly Father, thank You for today and the many blessings You've bestowed on us. We're so undeserving. Thank You for bringing Aubry home and for his love of Estelle. We thank You for their upcoming union. Be with them as they embark on this next chapter of their lives. Thank You for providing a job and a home. We will miss them, Father, but we know You will watch over them more carefully than we ever could. Thank You for this food, but most of all we thank You for Your Son who gave His life for us, a concept that has become more real to me since war overtook our world." Estelle's father's voice cracked, and he cleared his throat. "Help us to live every day to its fullest. Amen."

"Amen." Estelle mouthed the word as she raised her head and gazed at her father, the tears in his eyes bringing moisture to her own.

He squeezed her fingers before releasing them, then picked up the bowl of steaming sweet potatoes and handed it to her. With a lazy wink, he said, "Yes, your old man's getting to be a softie. What of it?"

"I like it." She plopped a dollop of potatoes on her plate, and passed the bowl to Aubry, who served himself, then handed the bowl to his mother. "To keep with today's theme, I want to say how thankful I am for everyone at this table. Mother and Daddy, you have worked hard to raise me, sacrificing all the while. I'm nervous about what comes next, but I know you've prepared me." She slid her gaze to Aubry's mother. "Thank you for accepting me into your family, making me feel like your own daughter." Next, she looked at Aubry, her true love, the man she would walk beside for the rest of her life. "And thank you for loving me, for your patience and understanding until I finally came to my senses. I will make it my goal every day to show you how much I love you."

"As will I." He picked up her hand and kissed her fingers, making the skin tingle.

Her parents and Mrs. DeLuca clapped their hands, their faces shining. Estelle smiled, her heart brimming. Her father was right. God had blessed them beyond measure in ways she could never have imagined when Aubry came home broken and bitter. Their life together would not be all roses and rainbows, but it would be filled with joy and love, and they would be thankful in spite of any circumstances that came their way, not because of them.

THE END

We hope you enjoyed **TEXAS WILDFLOWERS** and that
you'll continue reading all this year's
Thanksgiving Books & Blessings Collection:

Texas Troubles

by Caryl McAdoo

Raise up your children in the way they should go and when they are old, they will not depart from it. Getting the babies old is the key! Maisie Lowell and Rayne St. Laurent, each as beautiful as a wild Texas prairie rose, were born to privilege, reared in the fanciest hotel west of the Mississippi, and spoiled almost rotten--used to having their ways. In 1875 Dallas, Texas, the best friends determine to choose their own life paths to peace, joy, and love regardless of what their parents consider right or wrong.

New Beginnings

by Karen Gammons

Light, Love, and New Beginnings Replace the Sorrows of Her Past. Francis Lee lost everyone she ever loved to scarlet fever. Her landlord evicts, forcing her to go to Forlorn to live with her husband's cousin Sam and his family. She goes to be the new schoolteacher, and Sam's wife helps her find God's love and she meets another cousin, Joseph, but turmoil and jealousy at the fall festival makes her rethink things.

A Dark Lustre

by Amy Walsh

To join family in America, Emiliana crosses the Atlantic with hope. During the voyage, Austin, the Viscount of Marshallford, gains her admiration when he befriends the parents of her four young charges. To save his family estate, he goes to marry an American heiress, never expecting to fall in love with a penniless Polish nanny. Both find tragic circumstances call for desperate measures. If they ever meet again, how could she trust a man seeking an alliance with those oppressing her family?

Estelle's Endeavor

by Linda Shenton Matchett

Will a world at war destroy a second chance at love?

Estelle Johnson promises to wait for Aubry DeLuca to return from war, but then she receives word of his debilitating injuries. Does she have the strength to stand by him during his hour of need?

Aubry DeLuca storms the beaches of Normandy, then wakes up in a hospital, his eyes heavily bandaged. Will the only woman he's ever loved welcome him home or is he destined to go through life blind and alone?

All the Thanksgiving Books & Blessings Collection Stories

2018 – Collection One

Book 1: <u>GONE TO TEXAS</u> by Caryl McAdoo
Book 2: <u>GATEWAY TO THE WEST</u> by Susette Williams
Book 3: <u>TRAIL TO CLEAR CREEK</u> by Kit Morgan
Book 4: <u>HEATH AND HOME</u> by Pauline Creeden
Book 5: <u>NO TURNING BACK</u> by Lynette Sowell
Book 6: <u>DAUGHTER OF DEFIANCE</u> by Heather Blanton
Book 7: <u>UNMISTAKABLY YOURS</u> by Kristin Holt
Book 8: <u>ESTHER'S TEMPTATION</u> by Lena Nelson Dooley

2019 – Collection Two

Book 1: <u>TEXAS TEARS</u> by Caryl McAdoo
Book 2: <u>SPRING OF THANKSGIVING</u> by Liz Tolsma
Book 3: <u>THANKFUL FOR THE COWBOY</u> by Mary Connealy
Book 4: <u>THESE GREAT GIFTS</u> by Allison Pittman

2020 – Collection Three

Book 1: <u>CAROLINA HOMECOMING</u> by Heather Blanton
Book 2: <u>TEXAS TROUBLES</u> by Caryl McAdoo
Book 3: <u>A PINK LADY THANKSGIVING</u> by Donna Schlachter
Book 4: <u>MAGNOLIA'S METHODS</u> by Kimberly Grist

2021 – Collection Four

Book 1 – <u>TEXAS TIMBERS</u> by Caryl McAdoo

2022 – Collection Five

Book 1: <u>TEXAS WILDFLOWERS</u> by Caryl McAdoo
Book 2: <u>NEW BEGINNINGS</u> by Karen Gammons
Book 3: <u>A DARK LUSTRE</u> by Amy Walsh
Book 4: <u>ESTELLE'S ENDEAVOR</u> by Lind Shenton Matchett

Please enjoy a Sneak Peek at the next Thanksgiving Books & Blessings story!

Enjoy Chapter One of Texas Wildflowers

Dallas, Texas

Rayne blew on the page, filled her lungs, then smiled at what she'd written in her new journal—one of her favorite presents at her twelfth birthday party, probably because her best friend in the whole world gave it to her.

And there, scripted in her best handwriting, it existed in black and white . . . For all the world to see . . . if anyone got their hands on it.

What she'd known for a long time.

All that waited for her to do was help him to realize he loved her as much as she loved him.

Even though she adored Maisie—who probably wouldn't like it at all—she'd have to figure out a way to help her sister-friend get over it. Rayne chuckled. Her bosom buddy always did, no matter what.

She was confident the girl truly loved her and always had, just as Rayne loved her, every bit as much, more, truth be told.

She couldn't remember a time before the blonde beauty hadn't been there to play dolls with and climb trees with and ride horses with. Indeed, she loved Maisie Lowell! Just not as much as she loved her brother!

How many times had she or Maze said, 'if only you could be my real sister'?

Years passed; birthdays came and went, but Rayne's love for the young man waned not one iota. She filled three more secret journals, detailing her life so far, interspersed with her deepest hopes and dreams to marry him.

Those most important books, the only things that belonged solely to her, she kept in a secret place.

No one—not even Maisie—had ever seen or read one page.

Once upon a time, her father had belonged to her alone, but then Miss Priscilla Madison came all the way from Illinois and wrapped Quincy St. Laurent around her little finger—where she still had him.

He couldn't help falling in love with her more than anyone else could. The lady was so wonderful. Everyone fell in love with her.

Soon after she arrived, she married the Lowell House chef and become Rayne's stepmother and since, had been called Mama— longer than more than half her lifetime.

On occasion, Quincy's deep affections for the pretty lady tugged on his daughter's heartstrings and made Rayne jealous, but Mama made him so happy! She was grown up enough to share him.

Not her love though.

Three times, rumors swirled about one floozie or another, but nothing ever came of those vicious, tall tales. He was innocent! She hoped against hope he'd not even kissed any of them—so wanting her first kiss to be his, too.

Then as if he carried no regard for the condition of her heart, he got into a big fight with his father and left Dallas!

The Lowell House
Saturday, September 18th, 1875

Two more birthdays had come and gone for Rayne with neither hide nor hair of Baxter Lowell being seen and no one hearing from him that she knew of. Still, nothing short of him taking some other girl to wife would—or could—stop her from loving him.

Truth be told, she wasn't even sure that would stop her.

Surely she would love him for all of eternity!

Of course, she didn't sit home pining for him though—just in case.

Either he'd come home or not.

As every other fall dance at the Lowell House, Rayne and her mother had helped Maisie and Aunt Charity with all the exciting preparations.

Why, a body would think as prosperous as the Lowells had become—richer than anyone else in Dallas, probably all of Texas, she figured—they could hire it all done, but preparations proved at least half the fun of the event!

Her honorary aunt, Maisie's mother, always tried to outdo the year before.

With the dining hall decorated, all the tables moved out, and chairs lined up against the walls, leaving plenty of room for dancing, Rayne and Maisie retired to make themselves presentable and show off the new dresses Aunt Charity and Mama ordered from New York City.

It was plenty nice to have a home-away-from-home in the fanciest hotel in Dallas. Neither did it hurt that her parents worked there and were Uncle Morgan and Aunt Charity's special friends.

Growing up with her best friend Maisie being so close as long as she could remember—in the same hotel until she was eight before he married Priscilla—had been great.

As usual, the girl dithered too long over how she wanted her hair. Finally, Rayne twirled Maisie around from the full-length mirror, tucked a lock behind her sister-friend's ear then fluffed the sides. Here and there, she pinned in several tiny white carnations borrowed from an arrangement on Aunt Charity's desk.

"Ah! Perfect! Have a look for yourself."

Her friend turned around stared at her reflection for a moment.

"How can I argue? You're right! Do you want flowers in your hair?"

"Oh, no. I'm fine."

"Shall we go then? Mama hates it when we're late."

"Maisie Joy! We can't! Not yet! You know perfectly well it's fashionable to come to a dance last!" She flipped one of her curls as if above it all. "You know . . . as though you couldn't be bothered—then decided at the last minute to give the common folks the pleasure of your company."

"Why, if that Matthew Webb can swim the English Channel as he did last month, why not believe we can do anything?! Including getting to this dance on time!" The blonde giggled. "You and your high-falutin'! Now come on, Rayne Saint Laurent. Mama will switch us both if we aren't on time."

"She wouldn't dare! You're seventeen, and I soon will be! We are much too mature for corporal punishment."

"Still." More giggles filled the room with glee. "Let's not try her! She's been so moody of late!"

Baxter stood in the street, admiring his father's handiwork.

The Lowell House remained the grandest, fanciest, most expensive hotel in Dallas. His old home had the only elevator west of the Mississippi, plus forced air and ceiling fans to keep her guests cool in the Texas heat.

How many wagonloads of coal had it taken over the years to keep the steam engine operational?

"Sir, may I be of service?"

Baxter eyed the bellman, a fellow he didn't know. "The dance started yet?"

"Yes, sir. Most guests are . . ." The man looked him over hat to boot then cleared his throat. "Well, sir, it's a formal affair. I wouldn't want you to feel bad that you weren't dressed more appropriately. If I might suggest, there's another in the spring. Perhaps you could acquire suitable attire."

"For mercy's sake, man." He had to laugh. "Where did Papa find you?"

"Sir?"

More guests approached, dressed to the nines.

"I'm sorry, sir. I'm going to have to ask you to move along."

A man-sized shadow stepped into the gas light. "Baxter? What are you doing out here, boy? When'd you get back?"

"Deputy Tate." He tipped his hat at the lawman. "How've you and yours been?"

"We're all good. I'm not a deputy anymore though."

"I never would have thought you'd give up keeping the peace."

"Haven't. I work here now, at the Lowell House, head of
security. What are you doing out here in the street?"

Glancing back at his father's perplexed employee, he grinned.
"Oh, just admiring the old girl. Hard to believe it's been two years.
How come you're not at the dance?"

"Joseph here sent a runner for me."

He grinned. "Said an unsavory character was standing in the
middle of the street, looking like he might want to burn the place
down."

With a smile, Baxter glanced at the bellman then back to Tate.
"Once upon a time maybe. Your employer knows well how to
ruffle my feathers. Are he and Mama in fine fiddle?"

"Never better. Come on in. How does a bath and change of
clothes sound?"

"Have they moved anyone into my old room?"

"Not that I've heard about."

The music immersed his ears in fine culture as he walked
through the lobby to the ground-floor suite that had been his home
up until the last two years. Tate unlocked the door, opened it for
him, then stepped aside. "If you want, I can tell your father you're
here."

"Why not?" He grinned. "Come give me a ten-minute head start
though if he's still set on tanning my hide."

"Yeah, I heard about that." Tate grinned and winked. "I think
he's cooled off considerable."

"Mama talked him into any more books?"

"We're looking at several unsolved murders."

"I've got one for you. Have you heard about the preacher
getting shot in San Antonio?"

"Some, but last I heard they've got two men in jail."

"They didn't do it." Baxter leaned in close. "They were both at
a bordello I know of when the man got shot. Didn't say so on
account of their wives and the church folks."

"That isn't too smart."

"Especially since it came out anyway."

"Well, go ahead and get yourself cleaned up. Where's your
grip?"

"At the depot. Wasn't sure if I'd be staying. Any of the boys need a job? I'm looking for strong backs."

Tate laughed. "Doing what?"

"Laying track. I'm working for the railroad now, and we're hiring."

"How about that; I'll pass the word." The man pushed him on inside.

A shave and a hot bath hit the mark. Most of his old things didn't fit, so we went scavenging. His elder brother came through. Enoch had left some of his coats and trousers in a steamer. It took Baxter better than an hour, but he finally got himself to the main dining hall.

At least a hundred and fifty folks filled the room. His pater familias spotted him first and nodded. Well, that was good. His father walked toward his mother, who chatted with two older ladies. From behind her, he put his mouth to her ear.

Whirling around, she thew her hands into the air. "Baxter! My prodigal son! You've come home!" She hurried toward him.

A shriek sounded to his right. From across the room a streak of blond curls came flying his direction, leaving little flowers in her wake. A blue dress billowed. How could the young woman racing toward him be his little sis? Mercy's sake! He braced himself as she threw herself into his arms.

"Oh, Brother! You've come home!" Maisie had gone and turned into a grown woman while he traveled the world.

All in all, it appeared to be a much better reception than expected.

Oh, Sweet Lord! He had answered Rayne's prayers!

Though her eyes confirmed what she knew to be true—Baxter Reagan Lowell had come home—she could hardly believe it. Maisie had taken off full throttle and thrown herself into his arms, but Rayne couldn't do that.

A distance must be kept. Her heart beat so joyfully, he'd surely be able to hear if she got too close. She swallowed and pushed her keen excitement down as deep as she could.

Decorum must be maintained.

After all, she was no longer a child.

His last words to her before he'd left had stung every day he'd been away. She would not give him reason to repeat them! She took in several breaths . . . in, out, in, out . . . forcing herself to calm down. He couldn't know how he affected her—not yet.

Though longing to be at his side, she gave Aunt Charity and Maze time to greet him.

Finally, well in control, she strolled through and around the dancers to the happy reunion. The closer she got, the better he looked.

Oh, how he had changed! His shoulders seemed so much broader, and his chest, barreled. He glanced her way, and she gasped. He couldn't have heard it though, could he? He looked right past her as if he didn't even know her at all.

Just as quickly as his gaze had passed though, it returned to rest on her.

She smiled and floated toward him.

Aunt Charity and Maisie—his brother Enoch and Vi and all the other well-wishers—they all faded and disappeared from her vision.

Only her Baxter remained and what a sight he was!

"Rayne? Is it you?"

Not trusting her voice, she smiled and batted her lashes extravagantly. She pouted her bottom lip just a bit like the ladies did in the books she read before touching his forearm.

Some of his strength flowed from his forearm through her hand and then to her vocal cords.

"Where have you been? We've all missed you so much."

"All over." Movement turned his head; Uncle Morgan neared. She backed up.

"Great to see you, Son. Welcome home."

The men shook hands, then his father pulled him into an embrace. Good. Hopefully, the past wouldn't rear its ugly head. If she'd heard right, the big fight had been over Baxter not standing still for a whipping, but she and his sister were never made privy to the why of it all.

"Did I hear right? You're working for the railroad?"

Baxter nodded his handsome face, beaming. "Yes, sir. Matter of fact is . . . I'm part owner."

"Congratulations. How did that come about?"

"Oh, Papa!" Maisie horned her way between her father and brother. "We can hear all about that later! I want to dance with Bax, so leave him alone." She pulled him out a ways then held her arms out.

Rayne should have thought of that. But then most men didn't care much for forward women—at least that's what the older ladies claimed. The next tune, Baxter danced with his mother.

When that song finished, he kissed Aunt Charity's cheek then walked toward her with a silly grin she loved, as if he might be flirting a little.

He held his hand out. "May I have this dance?"

"Why, Mister Lowell! You certainly may." She took hold of his offering and he escorted her onto the floor, twirling her around then into his arms. Her heart took flight again. She kept a good arm's length between them, so perhaps he wouldn't be able to tell.

For the first full circle about the floor, she only gazed into his eyes, opening hers wide. Oh, how she hoped he would see her love for him overflowing in them.

"If I'm remembering right, you've got a birthday coming up next month."

"Yes, sir. Three months after Maisie's and two before yours."

"I thought so. I brought you a present."

"What? You did?"

"Yes, ma'am. You've always been like a sister to me."

His words stopped her heart from beating. Her first thought was to let go, get out of his embrace, and back away, but she maintained. Her cheeks flashed red hot; they had to be as red as a cherry!

"I . . . I . . . Well, I am not your sister, Baxter Lowell."

"What?" Shock twisted his face. "Oh. My apologies."

Why had she said that in such a nasty tone?

214

Oh, Lord! He would surely hate her after that little outburst. Not knowing what to say, she went with her first instinct. Pivoting, she dropped her arms, turned away, and forced her feet to take measured steps, as badly as they wanted to run.

Once out the door, she ran to the residence. Bless the Lord that she knew where the key was hidden.

Once in Maisie's room with the door locked, she threw herself across the bed. The trickle of tears that wet her cheeks on the way gave way to a flood.

What had she done?

The answer came easily enough.

She'd just ruined her life!

What did you think of *Estelle's Endeavor?*

Thank you so much for purchasing *Estelle's Endeavor*. You could have selected any number of books to read, but you chose this book.

I hope it added encouragement and exhortation to your life. If so, it would be nice if you could share this book with your family and friends by posting to one or more of your favorite social media outlets.

If you enjoyed this book and found some benefit in reading it, I'd appreciate it if you could take some time to post a review on Amazon, Goodreads, Kobo, GooglePlay, Apple Books, B&N, or other book review site of your choice. Your feedback and support will help me to improve my writing craft for future projects and make this book even better.

Thank you again for your purchase.

Blessings,

Linda Shenton Matchett

Other Titles by this Author

Romance

Love's Harvest, Wartime Brides, Book 1

Love's Rescue, Wartime Brides, Book 2

Love's Belief, Wartime Brides, Book 3

Love's Allegiance, Wartime Brides, Book 4

Spies & Sweethearts, Sisters in Service, Book 1

The Mechanic & The MD, Sisters in Service, Book 2

The Widow & The War Correspondent, Sisters in Service, Book 3

Gold Rush Bride Hannah, Gold Rush Brides, Book 1

Gold Rush Bride Caroline, Gold Rush Brides, Book 2

Gold Rush Bride Tegan, Gold Rush Brides, Book 2

Dinah's Dilemma, Westward Home & Hearts Mail Order Brides

Rayne's Redemption, Westward Home & Hearts Mail Order Brides

Daria's Duke, Westward Home & Hearts Mail Order Brides

Ellie's Escape, Westward Home & Hearts Mail Order Brides

Vanessa's Replacement Valentine, Brides of Pelican Rapids

A Family for Hazel, Brides of Pelican Rapids

Legacy of Love, Keepers of the Light

A Bride for Seamus, Proxy Bride Series

A Bride for Keegan, Proxy Bride Series

Love at First Flight

Love Found in Sherwood Forest

On the Rails: A Harvey Girls Story

A Love Not Forgotten

A Doctor in the House

Mystery

Under Fire, Ruth Brown Mystery Series, Book 1

Under Cover, Ruth Brown Mystery Series, Book 2

Under Ground, Ruth Brown Mystery Series, Book 3

Murder of Convenience, Women of Courage, Book 1

Murder at Madison Square Garden, Women of Courage, Book 2

Non-Fiction

WWII Word Find, Volume 1

Let's Connect!

www.LindaShentonMatchett.com

www.facebook.com/LindaShentonMatchettAuthor

www.pinterest.com/lindasmatchett

www.linkedin.com/in/authorlindamatchett

https://www.amazon.com/Linda-Shenton-Matchett/e/B01DNB54S0

https://www.bookbub.com/authors/linda-shenton-matchett

Interested in more historical fiction?

Visit http://www.lindashentonmatchett.com/p/books.html

ACKNOWLEDGMENTS

Although writing a book is a solitary task, it is not a solitary journey. There have been many who have helped and encouraged me along the way.

My parents, Richard and Jean Shenton, who presented me with my first writing tablet and encouraged me to capture my imagination with words. Thanks, Mom and Dad!

Scribes212 – my ACFW online critique group: Valerie Goree, Marcia Lahti, and the late Loretta Boyett (passed on to Glory, but never forgotten). Without your input, my writing would not be nearly as effective.

Eva Marie Everson – my mentor/instructor with Christian Writers' Guild. You took a timid, untrained student and turned her into a writer. Many thanks!

SincNE, and the folks who coordinate the Crimebake Writing Conference. I have attended many writing conferences, but without a doubt, Crimebake is one of the best. The workshops, seminars, panels, critiques, and every tiny aspect are well-executed, professional, and educational.

Special thanks to Hank Phillippi Ryan, Halle Ephron, and Roberta Isleib for your encouragement and spot-on critiques of my work.

Paula Proofreader (https://paulaproofreader.wixsite.com/home): I'm so glad I found you! My work is cleaner because of your eagle eye. Any mistakes are completely mine.

Thanks to my Book Brigade who provide information, encouragement, and support.

A heartfelt thank you to my brothers, Jack Shenton and Douglas Shenton, and my sister, Susan Shenton Greger for being enthusiastic cheerleaders during my writing journey. Your support means more than you'll know.

My husband, Wes, deserves special kudos for understanding my need to write. Thank you for creating my writing room – it's perfect, and I'm thankful for it every day. Thank you for your willingness to accept a house that's a bit cluttered, laundry that's not always done, and meals on the go. I love you.

And finally, to God be the glory. I thank Him for giving me the gift of writing and the inspiration to tell stories that shine the light on His goodness and mercy.